THE ROAD TO KENNESAW

"As the hart pants for the water brook, so pants my soul for you, O God."
Psalm 42:1 (KJV)

KAY CHANDLER
An award-winning author

This novel is a work of fiction. Names, characters, places and incidents are products of the author's imagination or used fictitiously.

Scripture taken from the King James Version of the Holy Bible

Cover Design by Chase Chandler

Dedicated

To my awesome, faithful readers at Grove Park Terrace, who continue to inspire me to be the writer God instilled me to be. Your friendship, love, and continued encouragement has been a tremendous blessing. I love you dearly and thank the Lord for placing each one of you in my life.

Surely, the Lord is in this place.

PROLOGUE

Nearby, Alabama
March 4, 1957

Rockwell Stone stared out the upstairs window of the Osceola Hotel and pondered how his life could've become so unraveled. For years, he blamed his troubles on the thorn in his flesh—his wife's mother. *But what if—?*

Rocky never got much further than the 'what ifs', and perhaps it was because he didn't want to believe it was his fault that things turned out the way they had. But what if he hadn't given Lilah an ultimatum?

He recalled the thrill he felt the day he signed papers to buy the quaint little cottage on Sandy Creek Road. As modest as it was, it was his, and for years, he struggled to pay for it. Located outside the city limits of Nearby—a little Alabama town aptly named for its proximity to the Florida beaches—the forty-acre plot wasn't good for much except for raising a few hogs. But it was all he could afford back in '41, when he wrote his name on the deed.

Though tiny and sparsely furnished, the little house on forty acres was his, and he couldn't have been happier if it had been Buckingham Palace.

Sixteen years ago, June 12, 1941, was the happiest day of his life, when he carried his bride, the former Lilah Jean Albertson, across the threshold. He bought a few hogs at the stockyards with the hopes of turning hog farming into a profitable business. He could have, too, if it hadn't been for his meddlesome mother-in-law.

Less than three months after the wedding, Lilah was in the kitchen frying bacon when she clamped her hand over her mouth and ran for the bathroom. Without two nickels to rub together, a couple of young and crazy kids were too excited at the time to worry about a war on the other side of the world. Lilah was four months pregnant when Rocky received the letter from Uncle Sam to report for duty.

The mixed feelings he had in '41 of wanting to defend his country, yet not wanting to leave Lilah alone, caused the familiar cramping in the pit of his stomach. He couldn't get past the fact that he was the one who suggested that Lilah's mother move in with her when he left for France. It was the stupidest idea he'd ever had. But how could he have known the woman would take over their lives and still be living with them, sixteen years later?

He and Lilah were ecstatically happy. . . for a season. But everyone knows seasons come and go. Rocky's season was far too brief.

When Rocky returned from the war, his mother-in-law was running the household with both Lilah and baby Cherub under her thumb, overruling anything he suggested. His wife had reverted into her mother's obedient child, and he had become an intruder in his own home. Over the years, the cottage he struggled to pay off became a prison for him.

He bought a few more hogs, but after much nagging from Lilah's mother, he eventually sold them and took a job at the local chenille mill. There was nothing he hated worse than being stuck in a building all day, but as much as he disliked his job, it was better than being home all day with the ornery old nag. The walls in the little house were thin, and with every passing month, his nerves grew thinner. The old woman parked herself in the living room with them every night until they went to bed. There was never a moment of privacy.

Rocky and Lilah had never fought until he suggested they move her mother back into her own home on the two-hundred-acre farm where Lilah grew up. It was a good house—solidly built, and certainly much nicer than the cottage. Sometimes he thought the only reason the old lady continued to stay at the bungalow, when she had a large, perfectly good farmhouse less than a couple of miles away, was for no other reason than to spite him. Anything she could do to make his life miserable appeared to delight her.

Over time, the hot anger churning inside him boiled over, causing him to lose control of his senses. In the heat of an argument and without considering the dire consequence of his words, Rocky spat out an ultimatum to his wife: "Choose your mother or your husband. You can't have us both. Either that woman goes, or I do."

It didn't go as he expected. Lilah's words cut to the quick when she blurted, "Rocky, I can't tell her to leave. She's my mama. If you can't live with her, perhaps you're the one who should find somewhere else to live."

And that was the beginning of the end. What if?

CHAPTER 1

Nights were the hardest.

Lilah Stone struggled to get through each long day, but the pain became unbearable in the darkness of night. She rolled over in bed, picked up the empty pillow beside her head and held it to her damp face.

She would never love another man the way she loved Rocky Stone. He understood her better than anyone, so surely he knew he'd asked the impossible of her.

At the first crack of dawn, she rolled out of bed and grabbed her robe. The aroma of bacon wafting from inside the kitchen made her gag. She recalled another time, when the smell of bacon caused her to throw up. But she was pregnant, then. There was no chance of that happening again. No chance at all. After running a brush through her hair, she trudged down the hall and dutifully took her seat at the table beside her daughter.

Dovie Albertson—also known as Big Mama for reasons which needed no explanation—appeared to be in an unusually merry mood. "Good morning, sweetheart. How would you like your eggs this morning?"

Lilah lifted her cup. "I'm not hungry, Mama. All I want is a cup of hot coffee."

"You have to eat, sugar. Cherie wants her eggs scrambled, so I'll go ahead and scramble yours."

"Mama, please stop treating me as if I were a child. I appreciate all you do for me and Cherie, but I'm a grown, married woman, capable of deciding whether or not I choose to eat."

Her mother gave a sarcastic chuckle. "Grown, maybe . . . but married? Really? Then where is he, may I ask?"

Lilah shuddered. The sarcastic question didn't deserve an answer. Her mother sat a plate of eggs in front of her, then preceded to give Cherie instructions before sending her off to school. Lilah picked at the eggs on her plate.

Dovie sat down at the table with a piece of toast and a glass of juice. "Looks like we might be fixin' to get some rain, today. Those clouds are really rolling in. I reckon I oughta put off doing the wash. What d'ya think?"

Lilah lifted a shoulder in a shrug. "Do what you want, Mama. You always do."

Ignoring the criticism, Dovie said, "Sugar, I've been meaning to ask . . . have you been by to see Coot since he got back in town?"

"Mama, please don't start."

"I declare, child, everything I say seems to upset you. I merely asked if you'd seen an old classmate. If you ask me, it would be the neighborly thing to do, to welcome him home, since you two were once . . ." Her voice trailed off.

Lilah loved her mother, but there was no denying the woman was everything Rocky had claimed—manipulative, controlling, hard as nails and intent on destroying their marriage. Could she blame him for walking out? Lilah's throat tightened. He offered her a choice, and she blew it. If she had to do it again, would she choose differently? Did it matter? It wasn't as if she'd get a second chance. Too many hurtful words had passed between them. There was no turning back.

****

There was a time when no one could've convinced Rocky Stone that he and Lilah wouldn't be together until death do them part. Now, things had progressed to a point of no return, and it was all his fault.

He watched from the hotel window as merchants on Commerce Street began to open their stores. Seemingly without warning, the blue sky turned the color of dark gray steel. A sudden white, jagged flash of lightening split through the heavens, just as Mr. Artie was opening his Barber Shop. A few seconds later, the sound of boisterous thunder rolled in, rattling the hotel window. The drops of rain came fast and furious, beating down on the tops of cars in a heavy downpour. It was then that Mr. Gil drove up and parked in front of the Jewelry Store. Rocky watched him open his umbrella, only to have the wind whisk it upside down. The elderly shop owner moved swiftly, belying his age, and in a split second, he was safely inside his store. Then, almost as quickly as it began, the rain slacked off to a slow drizzle and people went about their daily activities, as if the storm never happened.

Rocky's throat ached as he compared it to the storm in his personal life. If only it could be extinguished so quickly, and things could return to the way they were. How did he wind up alone in the Osceola Hotel, when everything he wanted was less than two miles away, all bearing his name? His wife . . . his daughter . . . and a little white bungalow with bright red shutters.

His eyes glazed over until the street scenes below became distorted. What if he'd kept his head instead of storming out of the cottage that night? What if . . . *if only*. It was his life's refrain—his punishment for allowing his head to rule instead of his heart. He despised the old woman, but living with her couldn't possibly be as devastating as living without his wife and child. He lumbered over to the bed and fell face down.

He should've known his wife well enough to know the ultimatum he gave her was one she couldn't live with. *If only—*.

CHAPTER 2

Dr. Sebastian Culpepper—known as Coot to those who knew him best—made all sorts of excuses for returning to his roots. However, he alone knew the real reason he gave up a thriving career at Vanderbilt Hospital to set up practice in his hometown of Nearby, Alabama. It was the words in a letter from sweet Mrs. Dovie Albertson, lamenting the fact that her daughter's husband had run off and left her.

Before he had time to stick the letter back into the envelope, he called a contractor in Nearby, inquiring about the time it would take to convert the old Culpepper home into a clinic—and to build him a nice brick home in which to live, atop Culpepper Hill.

The contractor stated that although he hadn't grown up in Nearby, he was familiar with the beautiful old home on South Commerce, known as the Culpepper House. "I'll look forward to getting together, sir. I'm sure the town will be thrilled to have such a prominent physician coming home to Nearby."

Things moved quickly, and about the time the azaleas began to bloom, Nearby had a new doctor in town, a clinic, and a gorgeous, ranch-style brick home on Culpepper Hill near the pond.

Dr. Culpepper's return to Nearby to set up practice made for interesting speculation. Some claimed he was kicked out of Vanderbilt Hospital and had returned in shame. A tale started that he was fired for taking out a child's appendix who had been admitted for a tonsillectomy, but that rumor was quickly dispelled when the source was revealed. Homer, the town drunk, should've been a fiction writer, the way he could make up stories.

Others hee-hawed at the notion that the doctor was fired, and said he simply missed his roots and wanted to return to the town where his deceased father and grandfather began practicing medicine. But the most interesting thought—and the one which continued to spread—was that he came back because of a woman he was once in love with.

The recently renovated medical clinic in Nearby became the talk of the town. The beautiful old Greek Revival home was still as lovely as ever, although once inside there was no mistaking it had been converted into a mini-hospital. The plastered walls reeked of the strong odor of antiseptics.

****

Dovie Albertson dried her hands on her apron and hung it on a nail. "Lilah, I'm tired of seeing you mope around this house all day. When will you wake up and realize you're better off without the scoundrel? If he really loved you, would he have left? Face it!

The man couldn't wait to get out of here."

Lilah sipped on her coffee, then mumbled. "That's not true, Mama. We both know why he left."

Dovie threw up her hands. "Good grief, Lilah, if it helps your feelings to blame me, then go ahead. But you know I only want what's best for you. What kind of mother would I be if I didn't?" She walked over and sat back down at the table. She reached over and laid her hand on top of her daughter's. Then looking her in the eyes, Dovie said, "Hon, it hurts me to see you like this. Maybe I should've told you sooner—but a little birdie told me that Coot Culpepper gave up a prestigious position at Vanderbilt Hospital to come back to Nearby because of a love interest." She snickered. "Reckon who that little birdie could be referring to, sugar?"

"I don't know, Mama, and I don't care. I'm not interested in Coot. I'm a married woman."

Dovie jerked her hand back and rolled her eyes. "You keep saying that."

"It's true. Rocky and I are separated, but according to the law, we're still married."

"Girl, you beat all. You're still a beautiful woman, and if I had that good looking doctor wanting to woo me, I'd be sitting on the courthouse steps before it opened, waiting to get a divorce."

Lilah's jaw flexed. "Stop it, Mama. Haven't you done enough damage?"

Dovie's tone changed, and it was obvious Lilah had offended

her. "I suppose it makes you feel better to push the blame off on me. If you've finished your coffee, get dressed and make yourself useful. I won't have you pining around the house all day, brooding over a hog farmer who doesn't care a flip for you or his daughter. The hinge on the bathroom door needs greasing and after that, strip your bed and wash the linens."

Feeling like a wind-up toy, Lilah dutifully dressed, walked out on the covered back porch, to look for an oil can inside the crudely-built cabinet, where Rocky kept his tools. She reached toward the small can of oil on the top shelf, when her focus shifted to a bottle bearing a red and black label, with an image of a skull and crossbones, but it was the word "Poison" that made her pulse race. Rocky had used it to kill rats. *What if?*

She picked it up and unscrewed the cap. Her heart pounded as she gazed at the light brown powder. Rocky always mixed it with cheese. The thoughts in her head frightened her.

Her mother yelled. "Lilah, what in tarnation is taking you so long to find the oil?"

Hearing the kitchen door slam, Lilah had no time to think. She quickly opened her mouth to pour the contents on her tongue. Her mother screamed and knocked the bottle from her hand.

Lilah's face scrunched into a frown as she stuck out her tongue and whispered, "Bitter. Poor rats."

Dovie screamed. "Open your mouth? How much did you swallow?"

Lilah's lip quivered. "Sorry, Mama. Tell Cherie . . ." Her

words slurred and she collapsed.

Dovie didn't have time to wait for an ambulance. She grabbed her daughter in her arms, carried her to the car and raced to the clinic. Pulling up in front of the door, she yelled for help, and within minutes, her beautiful daughter was having her stomach pumped with the hopes of keeping her alive. But no one knew how much poison was consumed before her mama knocked it from her hands.

After pumping her stomach, Dr. Culpepper came out and hugged Dovie as she wept. "Coot, how is she? Will she be alright?"

"It's too soon to tell, Mrs. Albertson, but you can rest assured, I'll do all I can."

"I know you will. You love her too, don't you?"

CHAPTER 3

Fifteen-year-old Cherub Stone heard all the gossip as she sat in the parlor-turned waiting room at the Nearby Medical Clinic. Why didn't people mind their own business? Who cared why the doctor left the big hospital in Tennessee and moved back home?

She rolled her eyes at a woman's suggestion that he was still in love with his high school sweetheart. He was an old man, for goodness sake—probably in his late thirties, or even early forties. Besides, what business was it of theirs if he was in love? The only thing that concerned her was her mother, and if he could save her, she'd be thankful he was back in town.

The waiting room emptied, and Cherub had never felt so alone. If only her daddy were there. He could always make her feel better, regardless of how bad things seemed. Had anyone let him know? Why wasn't she allowed to see her mama? Having counted the dancing prisms from the ornate chandelier three times, she rearranged the magazines on the table, then walked over to the water cooler, before trudging back to her chair and burying her face in her hands. "Why, Mama? Why did you do it?"

Her stomach wrenched as if she'd swallowed a bag of marbles. Anger, love, rebellion, hate, blame, and a headful of unanswered questions all intermingled like tangled threads, making it impossible to separate truth from lies. Her mother told her years ago that her father was the one who chose the name Cherub for her because he said it was a name befitting an angel. If he knew the thoughts swirling in her head, he'd want to change her name. Acknowledging the fact that her mother might never leave the hospital alive, the frightening thoughts not only made her sad, but angry that she'd possibly have no control over her life. No way would her grandmother allow her to go live with her father. What if the courts insisted she live with Big Mama? Shame added to her list of emotions. Cherub loved her grandmother. But was it so wrong not to want to live with her?

****

Rocky Stone ambled down the street to the corner drugstore, where a few fellows gathered every morning to swap fish stories before starting work. All four tables were taken, so he took a seat at the counter. He picked up the morning newspaper, which someone had left. While glancing over the ballgame scores he overheard whispers at a nearby table. His jaw tightened.

Swinging the swivel stool away from the counter, he jumped up and blurted. "Stop it, Gus. That's a lie. That's my wife you're talking about, and I know her better than anyone. Lilah would never do such a thing, so stop spreading your vile tales."

Gus shrugged. "Well, according to what folks are sayin', you ain't got no way of knowing, since they say she ain't your wife no more." Pointing toward the plate glass window, he said, "There's a payphone at the corner. Why don't you call the clinic and find out who's lying?"

Rocky stomped over and grabbed his hat from a nearby rack.

The mayor walked over and put his arm around Rocky's shoulder. "Aww, Rocky, don't let Gus ruffle your feathers. You know how he is. Shoot, we all know not to take him seriously, but hey, isn't it why we all keep coming back? You know how it goes: Someone comes in and says Lilah was seen going into the clinic with a stomachache from something she ate. And now, instead of a slight case of food poisoning, Gus has her gulping down rat poison." The other fellows at the table laughed and nodded.

Charlie said, "Hugh is right. Shucks, y'all remember when Gus claimed I won the lottery, and I wouldn't tell anyone because I was afraid y'all would try to con me out of it. That's one time I wish he'd been telling the truth. No one takes him seriously. Sit back down and finish your breakfast."

The mayor added, "Even if it's true that she went to the clinic, Dr. Culpepper has probably already given her a big dose of milk of magnesia and sent her home. Don't let Gus get your goat."

The mention of Coot Culpepper didn't make Rocky feel any better. Maybe the mayor was right, and he was making much ado about nothing. The fellows had a point. Without Gus's wild tales, the place probably wouldn't be as popular as it had become. And it wasn't shocking that Lilah might've developed food poisoning. Without question, her mother had more money in the bank than anyone in town, yet she held tightly to a dollar. He'd seen her scrape mold off of bologna and throw a hissy fit if anyone dared not eat it.

He stopped by the store and picked up a box of saltine crackers and a bottle of Ginger Ale, just in case there could be a hint of truth to the tale, and Lilah had eaten something that made her sick on her stomach. Besides, it would give him a good excuse to go by the house to see her.

Rocky swallowed the frog in his throat when he drove up to the bungalow, which had been his home for over sixteen years. He sat for several minutes, absorbing the view and reminiscing. He expected to see his mother-in-law come barreling out the door at any minute, swinging a sage broom and daring him to get out of the car. He chuckled at the funny picture in his head. Rocky got out, opened the gate to the white picket fence and recalled the fun he and Lilah had the day they painted it. Now, it needed another coat.

Walking up the stone steps, he glanced over at the porch swing and recalled the day they sat there discussing names for the baby. If a boy, they'd name him Steppen. Lilah laughed at first, but after repeating Steppen Stone several times, she agreed it was perfect. Lilah's mother insisted it was a girl because of the way

Lilah carried the baby. She insisted they name her Dovie Lou after her. He shuddered. Over his dead body. Not that Dovie Lou wasn't a perfectly good name, but he thought of people in the Bible whose names defined them. Like those twins, Jacob and Esau. One Dovie Lou was all the world could stand.

Rocky said only a name for an angel would be suitable for their baby girl. The name Cherub made him think of a cute little plump angel with short, yellow curls. He smiled, remembering the photograph Lilah sent him when Cherub was born, and she looked exactly the way he pictured. Missing out on his daughter's birth was one of his greatest regrets in life.

He knocked, but no one came to the door. Stepping inside, a flashback of memories accompanied by mixed emotions caused a tightness in his chest. Nothing had changed since he moved out, yet nothing looked the same.

Fond memories of him snuggling on the sofa in the tiny living room with his darling bride were quickly replaced with thoughts of a domineering woman sitting across from them in the cane-bottom rocker, barking orders, telling them when to eat, when to go to bed and when to rise. He supposed the thing that hurt worse was knowing Dovie Albertson never got over the fact that her daughter chose him instead of Sebastian—or Coot, as he was called while growing up in Nearby. Maybe Lilah agreed with her mama.

He swallowed the lump in his throat. Had she regretted marrying a hog farmer instead of the town's favorite son, the famed Dr. Sebastion Culpepper? What a stupid question. Of course she regretted it. Why wouldn't she? And if she hadn't been capable of thinking of enough reasons, her mother was there to help her think of plenty.

He walked around to the back, calling—first for Lilah—then for her mother, Dovie. Could it be Gus was right and that Lilah was sick enough to be admitted to the clinic? He got a wheezy feeling in his stomach. Picking up the phone, he called the Culpepper Clinic and asked if Mrs. Rockwell Stone was a patient there. Without answering his question, he heard the nurse yell, "Mrs. Albertson, telephone."

His knees buckled. When his mother-in-law answered, he said, "Big Mama, it's me."

"I'm not your Big Mama, Rocky Stone. What d'ya want?"

"I'm calling about Lilah. I heard she went to the hospital with an upset stomach. How is she feeling?"

"It's nothing to you. And don't come around stirring up trouble. The last thing my daughter needs is you showing up, causing a scene."

"Dovie, I need to know if—"

"We don't owe you an explanation, Rocky Stone. We got along before Lilah married you, and we can sure get along without you now."

The phone went dead.

****

Cherub stretched out on the settee in the clinic waiting room and thumbed through a Parents' Magazine, admiring the cute baby pictures. From the time she was old enough to play dolls, Cherub's one desire in life had been to fall in love, have six babies and live happily ever after, She wasn't sure why she decided on the number six, but looking back, perhaps it was put in her head the day she heard her mama tell a neighbor, "I don't think our little Cherie will ever be happy until she has a half-dozen young'uns. That child loves babies."

Mama was right. She hated being an only child and having a family of six kiddies seemed to be a good number at the time. But no more. No siree. She'd seen and heard enough lately to determine that marriage was not what it was cracked up to be, and no way would she put innocent kids through the turmoil she'd endured.

If Granny Stone was right and Hell really is a lake of eternal fire with screaming and gnashing of teeth, it was enough to make her try hard to be good. She'd heard enough screaming and gnashing of teeth to conclude that fire and brimstone couldn't possibly be any worse than the verbal accusations slung back and forth between her mama, daddy, and Big Mama. Nope. Marriage was no longer an option. She would never put herself nor innocent children through such agony.

Banishing all hopes of ever having a family, she weighed her options. Perhaps, she'd become a nun. Not that she knew anything about nuns, since she wasn't Catholic and had only seen one nun in her lifetime—but she supposed living a celibate life might get her a ticket out of hell, and with the thoughts she'd been having lately, she was likely to need it.

There was only one drawback. She liked boys. She'd been liking them a lot more this past year, especially since Molly told her that Tip Olds had a crush on her. Cherie supposed he was the cutest boy in school. Maybe the cutest in the county. The more she thought about it, she reckoned he was the best-looking fellow she'd ever laid eyes on. The thought of wearing a black habit day after day made her shiver. Besides, she loved sewing pretty new clothes, and she was good at it. What was she thinking? She'd never make it as a nun.

Swallowing hard, she tried to erase the insane thoughts swirling in her head. Did she really want to risk falling in love, only to wind up like her mother and father? If they couldn't make a go of a marriage that began with true love—and there was no doubt in Cherub's mind that they were once very much in love—then surely there was no hope for her.

She glanced at the tall grandfather clock in the vestibule. Two hours with no word. She was fifteen years old, for crying out loud. The hospital in Hartford, which was less than twenty miles away, would allow anyone over twelve years old to visit patients. Why wasn't she allowed to see her mama? It wasn't fair.

Cherub had fallen asleep on the settee when someone shook her arm. She looked up to see Granny Stone standing over her.

Jumping up, she grabbed the tall, thin lady by the waist, as her paternal grandmother's loving arms wrapped around her. Cherie loved both her grandmothers, but Granny Stone was much easier to get along with. She was sweet and softly spoken until someone got her dander up, and no one could do that as well as Big Mama.

Looking up with tears in her eyes, she said, "Granny, I'm glad you're here."

"I couldn't stay away, when I heard the news, sugar. I suppose your father is in the room with your mother?"

"No'm. He called the hospital, but I was standing there when the nurse called Big Mama to the phone. She told him not to come."

"I hope that means your mother is doing better?"

"Better? No ma'am." Her voice cracked. "Big Mama says Mama is gonna die."

Granny Stone's long, lanky arms tightened, as she leaned down and kissed the top of Cherie's head. "I am so sorry, darling. I know it hurts terribly to see her like that."

"But I haven't seen her. Big Mama won't allow me to go in."

"I see. Well why don't you stay put while I go take a look for myself? Your father will be here, shortly."

"No't, he won't. Big Mama told him not to come."

Her grandmother smiled. "That's how I know he'll be here shortly."

Cherub stood at the door and watched her granny walk down the hall and enter the door to her mother's room. Minutes later, she came out and stomped over to the nurse's desk. Cherub couldn't hear the entire conversation, but she was familiar enough with the personalities of both her grandmothers to know the encounter between the two had not gone well.

Granny Stone offered to take Cherie home with her, and she would have gone, if she hadn't been afraid her mother might die if she left.

****

Rocky sat in his car and took one backward glance at the bungalow, before heading to the medical center to check on his wife. He supposed Coot had learned by now that he and Lilah were separated. Rocky had often wondered if the reason Coot never married was because he'd never found a woman to take the place of his first love. Ridiculous. Sixteen years later and he was still jealous? He won, didn't he? Lilah chose him over Coot. He tried to make the marriage work. Anyone who knew him could vouch for that. He still loved his wife as much as he did the day he married her. Maybe even more.

But that mother of hers was more than any man could take. Well, maybe any man with the exception of Coot Culpepper. Rocky's jaw jutted forward, recalling how in high school, Coot would play up to the old goat. When Lilah was dating Coot, her curfew was eleven o'clock. When she was out with him, it was always nine-thirty. Rocky had always known the reason had to do with Coot being the son of the town's beloved doctor, whereas he'd never known his father. The gossip surrounding the mystery man who sired him didn't appear to matter to Lilah, but apparently it meant everything to her mother.

Dovie Albertson had been a noose around Rocky's neck the entire time they were married. But before he walked out, the situation at home had become unbearable. Every minute of every day was filled with thoughts of what he could do to change the distressing situation. He'd tried reasoning with Lilah, but they wound up saying hurtful things, which he was sure neither of them meant. Until a few weeks before he left, they'd never gone to bed angry. But before he walked out on their marriage, he was sleeping on the couch, and they were barely speaking.

CHAPTER 4

Rocky paused on the porch of the recently renovated Culpepper home, now known as Culpepper Medical Clinic, and straightened the newly placed shingle hanging beside the front door. The ornate letters carved into the oak placard read, "Dr. Sebastion J. Culpepper, M.D." Childhood memories of playing on this same wrap-around porch with his friend, Coot, caused an ache in his throat. He could still hear their voices in his head yelling in a sing-song fashion, "Ain't no boogers out tonight, grandpa killed 'em all last night." The little ditty made him smile.

Intertwining memories flooded back, as he attempted to separate the good, the bad, and the ugly. The childhood memories were the good ones. High School memories of fighting a rich kid for Lilah's affection were the bad ones. But living in the same house with a gripey, interfering mother-in-law who never allowed him a private moment with his wife was about as ugly as it gets.

His gut told him not to go inside. If Lilah had been admitted to the clinic, her ol' lady would be with her, and he was in no mood for a brawl with the woman. Ignoring the warnings in his head, he placed his hand on the gold knob and opened the massive front door, then stepped inside the vestibule. Everything looked as he remembered from his childhood. Maybe Lilah was really sick. But maybe she wasn't. Maybe it was an excuse for her to see her old beau, Coot. Rocky felt the blood rush to his head. Her mother would've certainly encouraged it. He had to know the truth.

What if Gus made up the whole cockeyed story about rat poison? It was a known fact that most of the rumors that circulated around town could be traced back to Gus McDowell.

If Lilah was seriously ill, wouldn't he have been notified? Though separated, they were still married. Rocky wanted to turn around and head back out, faster than he entered. Perhaps he would have if he hadn't seen his daughter sitting to the right in the parlor, staring up at him. He feigned a smile. "Hi, angel." He walked across the room and enveloped Cherub in his arms. "It's good to see you, baby."

The strange look on the fifteen-year-old's face reminded him of a frightened doe, facing the headlights. No doubt her Granny Albertson had turned his daughter against him, making her believe the split-up was all his fault. If he were honest with himself, maybe for once he'd agree with the old lady. Maybe it *was* his fault. Didn't Lilah give him a choice?

"Good to see you, too, Daddy. I didn't think you'd come."

"Why not?"

She shrugged. "Just didn't. Granny Stone was here but she left."

"Oh? I'm sorry I missed her. How's your mama?"

Biting his lip, he pretended not to see the tears welling in her big brown eyes.

"Big Mama says Mama is dying. Oh, Daddy, I don't want her to die." She burst into full-blown sobs.

Rocky pulled a handkerchief from his hip pocket and wiped her face. "Neither do I, sweetheart. But we both know your grandmother tends to exaggerate at times." He gently brushed a lock of hair from her forehead, while gathering his composure. "Let's pray that your Big Mama is being overly dramatic again, as is her custom." He desperately wanted to believe his own words and that whatever Lilah was going through was not as serious as her mother wanted everyone to think.

The fact that his wife was admitted for attempting to take her life made no sense. No sense at all and until he could hear it from the doctor's lips, he refused to believe it. A wave of nausea shot through him at the thought of Coot Culpepper being Lilah's doctor. Wouldn't Coot have even more reason than his mother-in-law to blow the situation out of proportion, so he could pretend to be the one in Lilah's debt for saving her?

Rocky grimaced at the crazy thoughts filling his head. He had to get a grip. That was years ago. They were all three kids. Water under the bridge, as the saying goes. Drawing a heavy breath, he reminded himself once again that Lilah made her choice. and she chose him over Coot. His childhood friend was not his problem. His problem was a meddling old woman who resented him from the day her daughter said, "I do."

Rocky tightened his lips, attempting to keep the angry thoughts from spilling into words . . . words which his vulnerable daughter didn't need to hear. But why on God's green earth would old lady Albertson say such a terrifying thing to a child, then leave her all alone in a waiting room to languish?

With his arm around his daughter, he said, "I don't want you worrying, Cherie. I'm sure it's not as serious as your grandmother wants everyone to believe. I do wish she would've called me when they first brought your mother in. She had no right to keep it from me. After all, Lilah is still my wife, but I had to hear it at the cafe that she was brought in for food poisoning."

Brushing his hand across his face, he said, "I'm sorry, angel. I shouldn't have said that. I'm as guilty as your Big Mama, for making you the whipping post. We have no right to take our frustrations out on you." With a head nod toward the door, he said, "Why don't we go down the hall and check on your mama?"

"Can I go?"

"Of course. Haven't you been in to see her?"

Her lip trembled. "Big Mama said it was best for me to stay in the parlor, that I didn't need to see her in such a state."

"Well, she's wrong. Of course, you need to see your mother. Just as I do. I suppose your Big Mama is in the room?"

"No sir. She walked with Miss Addy downtown to the café to get breakfast and said she'd bring me back a biscuit."

Rocky breathed a relieved sigh, glad that he wouldn't be forced to deal with an unpleasant situation, although he was prepared to do so if the occasion called for it.

Cherie lowered her head. "Daddy?"

"What, angel face?"

"I heard Big Mama tell Miss Addy that if you came, she was gonna make sure you couldn't go in to see Mama."

He forced a smile. "Did she, now? Well, I'm sure your mother wants to see you, sweetheart, and I need to see her for my own peace of mind. If Lilah doesn't want me to come back, I'll respect her wishes, but I'll be John Brown if I'm gonna let a third party dictate whether or not I can see my wife." He bit his tongue. He knew better than to badmouth his daughter's grandmother, regardless of what he thought of the old battleaxe. But it was difficult to keep his anger from spilling out. Reaching for Cherie's hand, he smiled. "Come on, let's walk down there together."

"Thank you, Daddy. I'm glad you're here. There's something else you don't know."

"What's that?"

"You said Mama was brought here for food poisoning. That's not true. Big Mama said she swallowed rat poison because she didn't want to live. I think it was my fault. She was upset with me for making a low grade in algebra."

So, Gus was right. This was one time Rocky wished he was wrong. He had a hard time keeping his composure. "Honey, I promise you, this isn't your fault."

Why would any grandmother choose to tell a child their mother wanted to kill herself, even if it were true. As they strolled down the long hall, Rocky tried to get his mind off the subject, lest he say more to the old lady than needed to be said in a public place. Taking his daughter's hand, he said, "This is the first time I've been in this house since Coot . . . uh, Dr. Culpepper, set up practice here. I assume the patients' rooms are all upstairs?"

"Big Mama says there are four upstairs, but two rooms on this floor for patients who aren't expected to live." Cherie's voice cracked. "She said the room they put Mama in was Dr. Culpepper's bedroom when he was a boy. It's a beautiful house, isn't it?"

"If you like this sort of thing." He clasped his lips together. What a stupid thing to say. Of course it was a beautiful house.

Rocky led his daughter past the library, then turned and walked down the hall to the second door on the left. He stood in front of the closed door, looked down and winked at his daughter. "Sweetheart, I know you're strong. You always have been. But today your strength may be tested. Do you think you're ready? Your mama may be sedated. I just don't want you to be frightened at what we may face."

"I was frightened when I wasn't allowed to see her. I'll be fine, Daddy, as long as you're here with me. But are you sure this is the right room?"

"You did say she was in Dr. Culpepper's old room, didn't you?"

"That's what Big Mama told me."

"Then, this is the right room." He gently pushed open the door. Rocky thought he was prepared for anything until he saw his precious wife, lying lifeless under an oxygen tent, the color drained from her face. His lip quivered. Had he done this to her? He whispered to his daughter, "Cherie, walk up to the bed and speak to her."

Her lips quivered. "Can she hear me?"

"I don't know, sweetheart. But if she can, she'll want to know you're here with her."

She tiptoed across the room, but just before reaching the bed, she turned, ran back into her father's arms and whispered. "I can't, Daddy. I'll start crying. I don't want Mama to see me crying. You go say something to her. Please?"

"It's okay, angel face. We'll go together." Walking up to his wife's bed, he reached down and took her by the hand. His heart sank, seeing she no longer wore her wedding band. He caressed her hand, then picked it up and kissed it. Leaning over her, he said, "Hey, Delilah." It was his pet name for her, although it had always irritated his mother-in-law, who would invariably correct him with, "I named her Lilah, and I'd appreciate it if you'd call my daughter by her rightful name." Maybe it was his imagination, or the aching in his heart, wanting to believe, but it felt as if she squeezed his hand. He gently squeezed hers and waited. Hoping. Praying.

There was no response. Why did he torture himself with vain imaginations? Rocky eased his hand away when the door opened. He relaxed, seeing a nurse instead of his cantankerous mother-in-law.

She walked over, straightened Lilah's pillow, and greeted her as if Lilah could hear every word. Then, turning to Cherie, she said, "You must be the daughter."

Cherie nodded.

"And you, sir? What is your relation to the patient?"

"I'm her husband."

Her brow shot up. "Oh? I'm sorry, but I've been given instructions that you aren't to be in the room. I must ask you to leave."

"And who may I ask gave you those instructions?"

"I probably shouldn't say."

"You don't have to. It obviously wasn't Lilah, since it's evident that she's in no shape to give instructions. But my mother-in-law has no legal right to keep me away from my wife."

"My instructions came from the doctor, sir, and he has every right to guard his patients when he believes it's in their best interest."

"You mean in his best interest, don't you?"

"I beg your pardon?"

"Never mind. I'm leaving, but my daughter stays in here with her mother as long as she chooses, and I dare you, the grandmother, or the doctor with all his medical knowledge and good intentions to object. Do you understand what I'm saying?"

"Yessir, you've made yourself quite clear. I see no reason for the young lady not to have visiting privileges, nor would I expect Dr. Culpepper to have objections. But I thank you for leaving."

"Before I go, I need to know. Is she . . . does she—?"

"She's in a coma, sir."

"Then she wasn't aware when I spoke to her?"

"No sir."

Rocky took his daughter's hand and walked her up to the bedside. "I'm going, Cherie, but stay here and hold your mother's hand. Talk to her, even if you're told she can't hear. We don't know that for a certainty."

Pleading with her eyes, Cherub whispered, "I don't know what to say, Daddy."

"Sure, you do. Talk to her the way you would if you were sitting at the kitchen table, shelling peas with her. Tell her about the things you and I talked about. Tell her how you had to rip the stitching out of the blouse you were making, but how beautiful it turned out. It's okay to complain. Tell her about you and your friend, Annie's squabble and let her know you need her advice, so she'll fight harder to get well. You can do that. Right?"

She nodded.

"And make sure you share with her about that *other* thing."

Her forehead scrunched into a frown. "Other thing? What other thing, Daddy?"

"You know . . . the thing about you being sweet on that Olds guy."

She let out a little squeal, then popped her hand over her mouth. "Daddy!" Then without denying it, she giggled. "How do you know?"

"I know my daughter. I can read your eyes. They flickered when you mentioned his name."

The nurse turned around. "Sir, you need to—"

"I know, I know. I'm leaving. I don't want to get you in trouble." Just as he started toward the door, he heard a faint whisper and turned on his heels. Had he only imagined it? "Was that Lilah's voice?"

Cherie burst into tears, shaking her head. "It was a nurse in the hall."

"I don't think so. It sounded like your mother said, 'What old guy?'"

Cherie snickered through the tears. "You're teasing. Mama didn't say that. She didn't say anything."

"Are you sure?" Rocky laughed out loud.

The nurse scowled, stiffened her arm and pointed toward the door. "Out!"

"Yes ma'am, I'm gone, but Cherie, sweetheart, didn't I tell you that your mama will want to know everything?" With a wink and a sideways glance at his estranged wife, he said, "Make sure you tell her all about the *old* guy, who's trying to steal my baby's heart."

A blush painted her cheeks. "Aww, Daddy, you're being funny. He's not old. He's only fifteen and his last name is Olds."

With a slight shrug, he said, "Sure, I know that, but your mother doesn't, does she? She wants to hear it from you. Talk to her, hon. She'll understand. She had a beau when she was your age." His Adam's apple bobbed. "In fact, she had more than one." Feeling the nurses hand on his back, he quickly kissed his daughter's forehead and left the room.

Halfway down the vestibule, he was reasonably sure he saw a man in a white coat dart into a side room. Had Coot seen him and chose to ignore him? It was understandable that even after seventeen years, the doctor was possibly still in love with Lilah. Why else would he use his authority to forbid Rocky from being in the same room with his wife? Would the same rules apply for any other couple? Not likely.

CHAPTER 5

After leaving the hospital, Rocky drove to the chenille mill. He dreaded having to go by the office to clock in. Granger, the supervisor, stayed on his back constantly, and the reason had nothing to do with his work ethics.

Granger was the quarterback in high school on a rival team. Rocky played quarterback for Nearby High. Nearby won the State Championship in the last fifteen seconds of the game, the year they both graduated, and Granger had held a grudge since then, as if Rocky had made the winning touchdown to spite him.

Granger looked up from his desk, then pointed to the clock without saying a word.

"I know. I'm late, but my wife is in the hospital."

"Your wife? Are you talking about Lilah Albertson?"

"Yes, My wife. She's ingested something that has made her very, very sick."

"That's too bad." He leaned back in his leather swivel chair and smirked. "Poison tends to do that. I heard this morning that Lilah had been admitted to the hospital for trying to commit suicide. What a pity. She's always been such a beautiful person. Seems I remember she dated Dr. Culpepper in high school. Some seem to think she's the reason he's back."

"She's still my wife, and her name is Lilah Stone. I just stopped to clock in and to let you know why I'm late."

"I don't give a pig's eye *why* you're late. The fact is, you've come dragging in here exactly one hour and ten minutes late. That's unacceptable. If I let you set your own hours, others will demand the same special privileges. You've been a fairly good employee, Rocky, but fair is not good enough. If you have any personal items here at the mill, I suggest you round them up and take them with you as you walk out the door."

"You're firing me?"

"Yep!"

"Fine. I have nothing here that I need or want. But before I go, I just want to say you were a fairly good quarterback in high school, but fair wasn't good enough, was it? 48-41. What a game!" He turned and walked away, slamming the door behind him.

He knew it was childish, but it gave him a sense of satisfaction, seeing Granger at a loss for words.

****

Cherub sat in a chair pulled up to the hospital bed and clasped both hands around her mother's. "Mama, if you can hear me, please squeeze my hand." When nothing happened, she repeated it once more. Her throat ached. What was the use? Big Mama was right. She should've stayed in the waiting room. Seeing her mother lying there lifeless, it seemed as if she were already dead. At the sound of the door opening, Cherie turned to look. "Big Mama!"

The stout woman's face scrunched into a frown. "What in tarnation are you doing in here, child? Didn't I tell you to stay put in the parlor?"

Cherie's first instinct was to admit she came in with her daddy, but knowing Big Mama would throw a fit, she simply said, "Sorry, Big Mama. I had to see my mama."

"Well, you've seen her, and little good it's done either of you." Pointing to her comatose daughter she said, "Do you really think this is how your mother will want you to remember her after she's gone?"

Trying to steady her trembling lip, Cherub shook her head. For a few brief seconds she had dared to hope, but those hopes came crushing down at the cruel finality in her grandmother's voice.

"I declare child, sometimes you can be as hard-headed as that no account father of yours."

"Big Mama, you have no right—"

"I have every right, sugar. Trust me, there are things you don't know and perhaps it's better that you don't. Now, scoot."

"Please don't make me leave. I'll sit in the corner and won't say a word. I promise. You won't even know I'm in here. It's boring sitting in the waiting room by myself."

"I'm sorry, but you aren't here to be entertained. If you're bored, then walk home and make yourself useful. The kitchen floor needs mopping."

"Big Mama, I want to stay close by in case—" The words stuck in her throat.

"Cherub, I know you're worried and I understand why you disobeyed, but hon, don't you think I have enough on my mind without having to worry about you, too?"

"Yes'm."

"Good. I'm glad you understand. Now, be a good girl and try not to give me any more grief than what I'm already having to bear. I honestly don't know if I can take much more."

Just as Cherub attempted to withdraw her hand, she felt her mother's gently tighten around her own. Her mouth gaped open. "Big Mama! You won't believe it, but she just squeezed my hand. I don't think Mama wants me to leave."

With a scowl, her grandmother was quick to admonish such a ridiculous notion. "Cherub, your mother has no idea you're even in the room, and she certainly isn't capable of reasoning!"

"But Big Mama, I felt—"

"For goodness sake, child, do you not understand why I need you to stay out of here? I can't deal with that imagination of yours at a time like this. You felt nothing. Do you understand? Nothing."

"But—"

Big Mama threw up her hands. "I said shush up, girl. I can't take much more. How many times must I tell you that your mother is in a vegetative state?"

"You keep saying it, but I don't know what it means."

"It means she feels as much as an eggplant would feel if you squeezed it."

Her jaw dropped. "Big Mama, that's mean, and it's not true. Does a vegetable have a heartbeat? Is there blood running through an eggplant's veins? Don't ever say my mama is nothing more than an eggplant."

"Hon, that's not what I said, and I'm sorry that it's what you heard. Lilah is not only your mother, but she's my only daughter and it hurts me to the core to see her like this. But if you're old enough to be in here, you're old enough to face reality, just as I've had to do. If you felt any movement, it was nothing more than an involuntary jerk in the muscles in my sweet baby's hand." Then reaching out with open arms, she said, "Come here, sugarfoot, and give your Big Mama a hug." Cherub knew her grandmother meant well, but resentment swelled within her. How dare she give up.

Big Mama wrapped her arms around her and matter-of-factly said, "I know you're hurting, child, and you don't want to believe it, but the sooner you accept the fact that your mama's mind is gone, the better off we'll all be. I have enough to worry about, without having to worry about your refusing to accept reality."

"But what if you're wrong? What if she really does know what's going on? I believe she does." Recalling her daddy's advice, she said, "Big Mama, I think she wants me to stay and talk to her. You know, the way we would if we were shelling butterbeans on the front porch."

"Cherub Stone, I've had about enough of your foolish jabbering." Then stretching her arm, pointing toward the door, she said, "You need to go to the house. Now! You aren't doing anyone a dab o' good by hanging out here."

Cherub jumped up. "I'm sorry, Big Mama, but I don't want to go home. I want to be close by in case Mama wakes up."

Her grandmother sucked in a deep breath, then exhaled with a long sigh. the way she always did when she was about to give in. Cherub waited . . . hoping.

"Aww, sugar, can't you see it's for your own good? This waiting can wear you out."

This wasn't the response she was hoping for. Cherub's voice cracked as tears trickled down her cheeks. "Please, Big Mama. Please, don't make me go home. I'll stay in the waiting room, I promise. Just don't make me leave."

"Suit yourself, girly, but trust me, you'd be much better off at home. Your mother could last an hour or two or a week or two, but if you insist on staying, you'll have to sit in the parlor. Now, scoot before the doctor comes in and sees you in here."

Her forehead crinkled. "I'm fifteen, Big Mama. Why would he care?"

"Are you gonna stall, asking silly questions, or do you plan to do as you promised?"

"I'm going. I just wondered—" Leaning over her mother, she reached down and kissed her cheek. "Big Mama, I think she's crying. Her cheek feels damp."

"It's sweat, sugarfoot. I'll pull the cover back. It is a mite warm in here."

Cherub shuffled back down the long hall. Then pausing, she debated whether to go home as Big Mama insisted or hang out in the boring waiting room. She loved her grandmother, although at times she wondered why. The old woman could never seem to find good in anything. Did all old people become crabby after fifty? Would she become an old grouch one day? With a sigh, she dismissed the gruesome thought, since Big Mama had been this way for as long as she could remember. But if it wasn't age-related, Cherie decided perhaps it was genes, which was just as disconcerting.

CHAPTER 6

Rocky drove over to the bungalow to pick up a toolbox he left behind. Now, that he was unemployed, he'd check at the Chevrolet Place to see if they could use an extra mechanic. A Jack-of-all-trades, he'd always been good at tinkering on automobiles. He was still driving the '49 Ford he bought at the sale over four years ago, and there was nothing under the hood he wasn't familiar with.

Seeing the grocery sack lying on the seat, he picked it up and carried it inside. He put the crackers in the pantry and the Ginger Ale in the refrigerator, thinking Lilah might need them after being discharged. A lump formed in his throat. *Is this what denial feels like*? He quickly rejected the thought and quoted a verse from the Bible. "They have not because they ask not.' Oh, Lord, I'm asking." He threw up his hands. "No, I'm pleading. Please, please don't take her away from me. I need my wife and daughter. Without them, I can't go on."

The linoleum floor in the kitchen was wearing thin in spots and would soon need replacing. Rocky looked around for other things that might need his attention. He fixed the spring on the screen door and the leaky faucet in the kitchen, which for a fleeting moment gave him a warm feeling that Lilah had needed him as much as he needed her, even if not for the same reasons.

He walked out, shut the door behind him, then noticed a car coming down the dirt road. Not just any car, but a shiny, two-tone, pink and white '55 Ford with fender skirts, white wall tires and a sun visor. He planned to own such a car one day. As it pulled into the yard, his jaw jutted forward. Coot Culpepper? Who else? Then recalling his mother-in-law making a point to tell him that the good doctor drove a new Cadillac, another frightening thought raced through his mind. Another suitor? Why should it surprise him? Lilah was a beautiful woman—but she was a beautiful married woman. She wouldn't . . . would she?

Before giving the stranger an opportunity to get out of the car, he stepped up to the window. "Looking for someone?" He felt his jaw flex as he waited for the answer.

"Could be. Are you the owner of this little cabin?"

"Who's asking?"

"Excuse me, my name is Arnold Amsterdam. And you are—?" The fellow seemed right congenial, and after looking him over Rocky concluded the short, pudgy man in his sixties had not come courting.

"Rocky. Rocky Stone."

"Nice to make your acquaintance, Mr. Stone."

Judging from his double-breasted suit and swanky silk tie, Rocky concluded whatever the fellow was peddling, he probably couldn't afford. "Look, mister. If you're selling something, I'm not interested."

"Not selling. I'm buying."

With a sarcastic chuckle, Rocky said, "Then you've come to the wrong place. I have nothing you'd want."

"Don't be so sure." Making a gesture toward the house, he said, "Are you renting?"

"No. I own it, but I don't live here."

"I know you own it. I was asking if you're renting it out?"

"Not exactly. Why don't you get to the point?"

"Sorry. I didn't mean to offend. I own Amsterdam Realty out of Birmingham, and I'm interested in buying this parcel of land."

"It's not for sale."

"I'm willing to make you a price you can't refuse."

"Sorry. Unfortunately, this place means more to me than it's worth."

The man pulled a check from his pocket and handed to Rocky. "Are you positive it means more to you than the amount written on this check? Everything is filled in, including your name."

Rocky stared at the figure. It was more money than he'd seen in his lifetime. "What kind of joke is this?"

"No joke. I have a client who has bought the Johnson Farm to your left and the Graham parcel to your right, but he can't proceed with his plans without your forty acres."

"And what, may I ask does your client plan to do with all this land?"

"He's an aviator and wants to build an airport."

Rocky laughed. "You must take me for an idiot. Anyone with that much money is too smart to throw it away on an airport in this little town. I doubt there are more than a half-dozen folks within a hundred miles of here who have ever been or would even choose to fly in a plane. Now—what do you really want it for?"

"Are you saying you can't use the money?"

Rocky looked back down at the figure on the check. "How do I know it's good?"

"You can follow me to the Bank, but I suggest you have the deed in hand, because I have a feeling you'll change your mind about selling a little shanty on forty acres of sandy soil."

Convinced the man was lying, yet out of curiosity, Rocky would play it out. "Fine. The deed is not here, but I'll go get it and meet you at the bank."

Mr. Amsterdam grinned and reached out his hand. "Just in case you decide to be one of the few people in town who might like to take off in a plane, I'll hold the check until you produce the deed."

Rocky handed the check back to him and grinned. "No problem. See you in a bit." He drove away, smiling at the strange encounter. The guy was nuts. What was he trying to pull? No one was that stupid, yet curiosity wouldn't allow him to forget the strange encounter. He drove over to the hotel, took the elevator to his room, pulled the deed from a bureau drawer and stuck it in his coat pocket. Rolling his eyes, he mouthed the words, *An airport, indeed.* But what if? Perhaps Mr. Amsterdam wasn't the only stupid fellow in the County, but why not play it out?

As soon as he rounded the corner on Commerce Street, the first thing that caught his eye was the '55 two-tone Ford parked in front of the Citizens Bank. No way was the fellow really going to pay such an outlandish sum of money for forty acres of land. Yet, his heart pounded at the mere thought of, "What if?"

Walking into the bank, he spotted Mr. Riddles, the bank President standing there with Mr. Amsterdam and Lon Guilford, the local attorney. Mr. Riddles motioned for Rocky to follow them into his office.

After thirty minutes of convincing him that the transaction was indeed valid, Rocky pulled the deed from his pocket, handed it over and deposited a sum of money that was more than he could've hoped to make in ten years. Maybe twenty.

His first act of business was to hire a guy with a truck to move Dovie's furniture from the cottage and set it up in the Albertson homestead. His heart fluttered. If his prayers were answered and Lilah woke up, at least now he had something to offer her, and her mother would already be living in her own house.

Then reality set in. What if she didn't wake up? The money

would mean nothing.

****

Coot regretted not telling Lilah how he felt about her when he first returned. Perhaps if he had, she wouldn't have made the attempt on her life. He remembered a time when she had feelings for him, too.

Coot spent a great deal of his time consoling Lilah's precious mother. Mrs. Albertson had always been good to him—treated him like a son. It grieved him deeply to see her in such pain. He hung his head. "Mrs. Albertson, I know you're hurting. I wish I could tell you that she will wake up and be her same sweet self. Unfortunately, at this point it doesn't look good. But I promise you that I'll do everything in my power to bring her back to us."

Pushing up from her chair, Dovie yanked on her girdle, then waddled to the other side of the hospital bed with her arms outstretched. "Bless your heart, Coot, you should've been the one to walk her down the aisle. If it had been you, she wouldn't be in this fix."

Embracing the woman, he said, "I know you mean well, Mrs. Albertson, but Lilah made her choice and regrettably for me, she chose my best friend. Maybe one day I will find someone who will love me as much as she loves Rocky."

"Fiddlesticks. I live with her, and I happen to know her better than anyone. She doesn't love that man."

He pushed back. "I know you're saying that to appease me, but I'm sure you're wrong."

"I wish I were, because her happiness means the world to me. However, I certainly understand why she feels as she does. Coot, I can tell you a lot that you don't know but pardon me, please, while I sit back down. These milk legs are killing me."

He glanced down at her swollen ankles. "You don't seem to understand how true that statement is, Mrs. Albertson. You're ignoring everything I've told you to do. You should be home with your legs bandaged and propped up. There's really no need in your staying here at the hospital. If there's any change, I'll notify you immediately."

"Oh, Coot, how can I stay home when my only daughter is at death's door?"

"Well, you aren't helping her by putting your own health at risk. I care for your daughter, and I promise I'll keep a watchful eye on her."

"Bless your heart, Coot. I know you loved her, and I'm so sorry the way things turned out."

"*Loved* her? I still love her, Mrs. Albertson. I've never loved anyone else." Lowering his head, he said, "I'm sorry. I had no right to say that."

Rubbing her hand across his back, she said, "Son, you didn't say anything I didn't already know. I would've given anything if she'd married you." Heaving a heavy breath, she added, "But our sweet Lilah was young and impulsive at the time and the only reason she married the scoundrel was to spite me."

His brow lifted. "I'm sure that's not true."

"But it is. We'd had an argument the same day that she ran off with him. I love my daughter, but there's no denying she can be impulsive at times. Her father was like that."

"She's never gotten over you, Coot."

He chuckled as if he'd heard a joke. "I'm sure you're wrong, Mrs. Albertson."

"Wrong? If she had a reason for wanting to live, would she have tried to take her life? You've admitted we have no way of knowing whether or not she can hear. Talk to her Coot and let her know you still love her. If there's the slightest chance she can hear, your words could do more for her than all the medicine in this place."

With his lips clamped tightly, he shook his head. "I couldn't do that, ma'am."

"Why not? You're the only person who can give her hope. Let her know you love her as much as she loves you."

He hung his head. "Mrs. Albertson, even if I should choose to, surely you haven't forgotten that when a man says romantic things to a woman, he prefers to do so in private."

Dovie Albertson's jaw dropped. "Well, of course." Placing her palm over her grin, she said, "I was just leaving. Please excuse me, doctor."

Waddling up to the nurse's station, she announced that the doctor had requested complete privacy and wished for any calls to be held until he was ready to exit.

Cherie spotted her grandmother and rushed up to the nurse's desk. "Is there any change in Mama? She's . . . she's still alive . . . isn't she, Big Mama?"

"Calm down, girlie. There's nothing to report." She grabbed her granddaughter's hand. "Come on, sugar, let's go home. Your mama is in good hands."

CHAPTER 7

Rocky was waiting on the porch of the empty bungalow at a little past five o'clock, when Cherub and her grandmother returned from the hospital. He braced for the fight that was sure to come.

Before they reached the first step, he stood, shoulders back, legs slightly apart. Clearing his throat and in a strong, authoritative voice, he announced, "Big Mama, you don't live here, anymore."

With her hands propped on her bulging hips, she snorted. "Zat right? And you think that upsets me? For your information, that would suit me fine. You think I like living in this dump?"

"It appears to be so, since you've made it your nesting place for going on two decades."

Her brow lifted. "Only two? Living with you all those years made it seem much longer."

"Not only to you, Big Mama, but to both of us."

"I'm not your Big Mama, Rocky Stone. But the day you hire a truck to come move my things, make sure you give the movers instructions to load my daughter's and my granddaughter's things, as well. The only reason I moved in this cracker box almost sixteen years ago was to care for Lilah, after you took off and left her expecting a new baby. Since she wouldn't move to the farmhouse, I stayed because she needed me."

"I took off and left her? You sound as if I deserted her. I went to war, woman. If I had known you were planning to—" What was the use in arguing. He should be grateful she was willing to go peaceably instead of putting up the fuss he'd come to expect from her.

She stomped up the steps, opened the front door and squealed. "What's the meaning of this?"

"What are you referring to?"

"You know what I'm referring to. My sofa and rocker are gone. And . . . and . . . Rockwell Stone, what have you done with my belongings?"

Cherub tugged on her grandmother's arm. "Big Mama, Daddy told you that—"

"Shush up, child. I'm talking to your father."

Rocky smiled. "Cherie was reminding you of your own words, when you said you were thrilled to be getting out of this—I believe you called it—a cracker box?"

"Well, you have no cause to throw me out. I plan to leave in my own good time."

"I think this is a very good time, especially since the house and the land it sits on now belongs to someone else."

"What are you talking about?"

"I'm saying I sold the place. It's now in someone else's name."

"You're lying to me. To begin with, who would want this heap?" She stomped into the bedroom. "You removed my bed? What have you done with my things, Rocky? I could have you arrested for this."

"For sending you back to your own home? You'll find everything you own in the farmhouse. I should've done it years ago. It's time for you to go home, Dovie."

With questioning eyes, Cherub looked up at her father. "What about me and Mama, Daddy? Where will we live?"

"Sweetheart, it's best you go with your granny for the time being, and by the time your mother gets out of the hospital, I hope to have a house for the three of us."

His mother-in-law growled. "Why torment the child with false hopes? My daughter will never set foot out of that hospital, and you know it as well as I. But don't you worry, Cherub, you'll never have to live with that man. I'll die first. He's the reason your mother tried to take her life. I won't let him destroy you the way he's destroyed her."

Cherie's lip quivered. "Daddy?"

Rocky watched with tears in his eyes as his daughter stepped into her grandmother's Studebaker. How he wanted to stop her, but it wasn't the time. The less trouble he caused now, the easier it would be for them both, later. The old woman had a lot of influence and could make trouble for him if he didn't handle things correctly.

But there was one thing of which he was certain. He loved his wife, and she loved him. All the trouble in the marriage had been caused by her overbearing mother who had hated him from the first date he had with Lilah. He and his best friend, Coot Culpepper competed for her affection all through high school, and though he never understood it, Lilah had chosen him.

Having the old goat interfering in their marriage had managed to drive a wedge between him and Lilah, who felt caught in the middle. He could understand why she tried to end her life. He'd felt like it sometimes, himself. Dovie Albertson managed to constantly keep something stirred between them, twisting his words to turn Lilah against him. *If Lilah lives* . . . He bit his lip. What was he thinking? He couldn't allow such negative thoughts to seep in. Though he still found himself jealous of Coot, Rocky had the peace of mind that no doctor would try harder to keep her alive.

He drove back to the hotel, threw himself across the bed and wept. He needed his wife. He needed his daughter. But the one thing he didn't need in his life was a meddling mother-in-law. Feelings that he'd never had before began to make their way into his consciousness. Wicked thoughts. Plans to rid himself of the influence of an evil old woman. Shivering that he could entertain such bizarre thoughts caused him to jerk straight up in bed. Then falling to his knees, he began to pray the Lord's prayer: *"Our Father, which art in Heaven, hallowed be thou name. Thou kingdom come, thou will be done in earth as it is in Heaven. Give me this day, daily bread and forgive me of my trespasses, as I forgive those who trespass against me. And lead me not into temptation but deliver me from evil."*

Rocky cried out, "Yes, Lord, please deliver me from that evil Dovie Albertson. She has been a noose around my neck from the first day I married her daughter. If only she were dead, but the old hag will probably outlive me for spite—"

He clamped his lips shut. Hearing his thoughts verbalized shocked him. Would God hold it against him?

****

Dovie Albertson held to her granddaughter's arm as she hobbled up the steps to the old farmhouse. "Ah, it's good to be home again. The place is a bit rundown, but with your help, sugar, we can get it all prettied up, just the way it looked when your PawPaw was alive. To tell the truth, I'm glad your daddy moved us out. I detested living in that cracker box he bought when he and Lilah married, but I couldn't talk your mama into leaving."

"If you hated it so much, why did you move in with them, Big Mama,."

"I did it for my Lilah's sake. She was determined to live there, and I couldn't bear the thought of her living with that man alone."

"Why?"

"Because of that temper of his, I was afraid of what he might do to her."

"He wouldn't hurt her. Daddy wouldn't hurt no one, Big Mama. I don't know why you talk like that."

"Just because he hasn't, doesn't mean he's not capable of it. Bless Lilah's heart, she tried her dead-level best to make that marriage work but thank goodness she finally saw the light and kicked the bum out."

"Big Mama, I don't know why you don't like my daddy."

"I'll tell you why. It's because he didn't care one iota about either of you, and it broke my heart. You both deserved more."

"You're wrong, I know he loves me."

"Oh, sugar, for your sake, I wish that were true. But Rocky Stone only loves one person, and that's himself. He uses everyone else. If he really loved you, why would he have moved your things out with mine, instead of moving you in with him?"

"Because he—" She choked, realizing she didn't have an answer.

"Honey, I know it hurts to face reality, but you're a big girl, and I refuse to hide the truth from you any longer. Now, why don't you go to your room and put up your things? If you like, I'll buy a gallon of paint tomorrow and you can paint it any color you wish. I'll hang some pretty white organdy Priscillas over the windows. It'll be so much prettier than that tiny room at the cottage."

Cherub fought back the tears. She should be grateful for all Big Mama was doing to try to make her feel better, but the only thing that could help her feelings would be for things to be the way she remembered them, when her mama and daddy were together. And since that was impossible, she'd never be happy again. Not ever. The longer she dwelled on her grandmother's words, the more she realized how blind she'd been. Big Mama was right. If her daddy really loved her, wouldn't he have wanted her to be with him? Tears flowed from her eyes. Well, if he didn't need her, why should she need him?

Dovie Albertson held her arms open wide. "Come over her, sugar, and let your old granny dry those tears and give you a big hug. Lord knows, it hurts me to see you like this. I could wring Rocky Stone's neck for the way he's treated you and your mama."

Wiping her face with her sleeve, Cherie shook her head. "I'm fine, Big Mama. I wanna go unpack my things."

"That's a good idea. You can take the room upstairs next to mine, sugar."

"Thank you, but I want the downstairs room that was Mama's when she was growing up."

"Suit yourself, but I'll need to get my sewing stuff out of there tomorrow. Don't reckon there's a reason I can't turn the upstairs bedroom into a sewing room."

****

Dr. Culpepper walked into Lilah's room and picked up her chart hanging at the foot of his bed. Glancing up at the nurse, he said,

"It's almost three o'clock, Nurse Adams, and we have nothing scheduled for this afternoon. Why don't you go home?"

"Then I'll be back at eleven tonight to sit up with her."

Coot tried to pretend Lilah Stone was just another patient, but his heart wouldn't allow him to forget. Where did he go wrong? As fond as he was of her mother, in a way he couldn't help wondering if it was Mrs. Albertson's fault that Lilah chose to marry Rocky instead of him. In trying to keep her daughter away from Rocky, Coot had a hunch she may have pushed her in his direction.

A lump formed in his throat. If only he hadn't been away at med school, perhaps he could've talked sense into her. Coot liked Rocky. Everybody did. Everyone except Lilah's mother. In high school he was handsome, athletic, and fun to be around. He was voted Most Popular Boy, beating Coot by only one vote. He still wondered if that one vote was cast by Lilah.

Mrs. Albertson's words played over and over in his mind. If he could only bring her out of the coma, he might get the chance he'd always wanted. Yet, with all his medical training, he felt completely helpless. There were cases where people claimed to have been aware of their surroundings while in a comatose state, but Coot found it difficult to believe. Yet, what if? What if he should tell her exactly how he feels? What could it hurt?

He stood and leaned over her still body. Stroking her forehead, he poured out raw feelings that had haunted him for years. Perhaps it wouldn't hurt so much if he hadn't felt he should've fought harder for her. Choking back the tears, he said, "Sweetheart, please wake up. I need you in my life. I promise you'll never have another reason for wanting to die. I can make you happy. I know I can."

How he longed for her to open her eyes and tell him she never stopped loving him. She looked as beautiful as she did the day he escorted her to the Homecoming Dance. He smiled recalling the awkward moment when he attempted to pin the orchid corsage on her lavender strapless dress. He remembered walking her to the door after the dance and kissing her under the porch light. It was their last kiss. She wrote him a note a week later saying she was breaking up with him. He didn't have to ask why.

With his forefinger and thumb, he lifted a curl from her forehead. He lowered his head and gently kissed her gorgeous lips. It wasn't planned. It just happened. Perhaps he should feel a sense of shame, but he didn't. Then lying his head next to hers, he caressed her cheek and eventually drifted off to sleep holding her hand.

"Doctor?" Coot jerked around at the sound of the nurse's voice.

Looking stunned, she said, "What's going on?"

He jumped to his feet and felt the blood rush to his face. "Miss Adams, I assure you there is nothing—nor has there been— anything going on, as you seem to suggest, and I'd be obliged if you wouldn't be so quick to judge. Frankly, I find it very offensive that you could make such an insulting supposition. I'm sure you understand how that kind of filthy insinuation could ruin my career."

"Doctor, the reason I asked, was because when I saw—"

"Stop!" He thrust his palm forward. "I don't care what you thought you saw. The truth is, Mrs. Stone is my patient, and I pulled my chair close, in order to sit nearby, hoping to observe even the slightest signs of improvement. It's been a long day, and I'm afraid my head must've hit her pillow when I fell asleep." He sucked in a quick breath, then blurted, "There is no other explanation, and I shall insist on your confidentiality." His words were running together, yet he couldn't seem to stop. "I can only imagine how others could misconstrue my intentions if you were to ever mention this unfortunate incident. Nothing improper happened. Do you understand? Nothing. Only a depraved mind would make something out of what you observed."

"Dr. Culpepper, I think you misunderstood what I meant when I asked what was going on. When I walked in and saw your compassion for one of our patients, I was touched. I wasn't judging you. I assumed our patient had experienced an episode of some sort and that you were keeping a close watch and ultimately fell asleep, just as you said. Borrowing from a Shakespeare quote, 'methinks the doctor doth protest too much.'"

"Are you calling me a liar, Nurse Adams?"

"Were you calling me judgmental? There was no reason to be so defensive unless what I saw when I walked in was worthy of such a lengthy justification. But for your information, sir, I have no reason nor desire to reveal the scene nor this conversation with anyone. I'm here to do a job and I'm ready to take my watch."

"Is it eleven o'clock already?"

"Close enough. Go home, doctor. It's obvious you need the rest."

CHAPTER 8

At the crack of dawn, Rocky left the hotel on his way to the hospital, while rehearsing the words he intended to say to his wife. He knew Lilah couldn't hear him, yet he had to say it. Maybe if he could tell her while she was still asleep, the words would be easier to say whenever she emerged from the coma. *She will emerge. She will.* Realizing it would soon be daylight, Rocky ran the remainder of the way, hoping to arrive before the doctor caught him there.

Easing the front door open, he tiptoed down the hall and made his way into Lilah's room. The nurse was stretched out asleep on a chaise lounge. He eased up to his wife's bed, leaned over and kissed her forehead. "Lilah, Honey, it's me. I'm back and nothing or no one can ever make me leave you, again. When you wake up from the coma, we'll start over. Just the three of us. Me, you, and Cherub." His voice broke and he poured out his heart, saying all the things he'd practiced earlier, and then some. The words were spilling out faster than he could think. He told her about the fellow who bought the cottage and the plans he had for them. "You remember how your mother constantly complained about living in the cottage and how she missed the farmhouse? Well, she's moved back and I'm sure she'll be happy, although we both know Big Mama will complain about the furnishings in heaven, if she ever gets there."

The nurse stirred. "What's going on? Who?" Then sitting straight up, she rubbed her eyes and gasped. "Mr. Stone, what are you doing here? You know the doctor has forbidden—Oh, my goodness, I'm gonna be in so much trouble if he comes in and finds you here. Please go." Her lip trembled. "I could lose my job over this. He'll fire me and he'll have every right to do so."

Rocky winked. "Calm down, I'm leaving. He never has to know." Walking down the hall, he heard a car drive up. He sucked in a deep breath. "Caught!"

He waited for the front door to open. The doctor stepped inside, then stopped short. "What are you doing here?"

"I came to see my wife, Coot. She is still my wife, you know." Rocky looked back and saw the nurse standing in the hall, waiting for his response. He quickly added, "And if it hadn't been for that nurse, maybe I could've accomplished what I came for."

"Rocky, I've asked you not to come here, and if I have to get a court order to keep you away from my patient, I won't hesitate to do so."

"That won't be necessary. I'm leaving." As Rocky reached the door, he heard Coot say to the nurse, "Well, done, Nurse Adams.

He can be persistent, but I appreciate your standing up to him."

****

As difficult as it was, Rocky managed to stay away from the hospital for almost two weeks, since Coot had threatened to have him locked up if he showed up there again. He missed Cherub, but as many faults as ol' lady Albertson had, he knew she loved her granddaughter. The hotel was no place for a kid, and for the time being, leaving her with Dovie was his only option. He called the hospital first thing every morning, only to be told there was no change. He wanted to believe it was a good thing.

Thursday afternoon he called once more to inquire about his wife but was given the brush off. After pushing for a report, the woman bluntly said she was not permitted to give out the information. He dismissed her rudeness and decided to look for himself on his lunch hour.

But as he was getting dressed to go to the drugstore for a cup of coffee and a doughnut, the phone rang.

"This is Shelly Greene from Greene Realty. Is Mr. Stone available?"

"Rockwell Stone, speaking. What can I do for you?"

"It's what I can do for you, sir. I think I've found exactly what you've been looking for. It's a two hundred and fifty acre horse farm, just outside of Bonifay. The previous owner just died, and his wife plans to move to Jacksonville to be near their daughter. I realize you're a hog farmer, but you might wish to go in a different direction after you take a look at the house and stables. It's a dream package. The price is set for a quick sale."

"I'm interested. Where shall I meet you?"

"What about the little grocery store at the corner of Hog & Hominy Road?"

"Perfect. I can be there in thirty minutes."

The realtor was waiting when he arrived. As they approached the destination, his eyes watered. Surely God had done exceeding abundantly more than he could've ever asked or hoped for. He could remember driving past and having seen a few horses grazing. But as many times as he'd driven down that stretch of highway, he'd never paid attention to the gorgeous home, surrounded by acres of beautiful white fencing. He supposed one seldom pays attention to things outside their reach, and certainly until now, this horse ranch would've been more than he could've ever hoped to own. Although he waited to complete the tour with the realtor, he could've told her before he ever stepped foot outside his car that he was ready to sign the papers.

"Well, Mr. Stone, do you have any questions?"

"Yes. Where do I sign?"

She laughed. "I thought you'd say that. If I had the money, I would've bought this place myself. It's a dream come true, am I right?"

"I don't know. I've never allowed myself to dream this big."

"I suppose since you didn't bring your wife, you hope to surprise her?"

"Yes. That's exactly right. Surprise her. That is indeed my hope."

She assured him she'd have all the papers drawn up by morning and since he was paying cash, she said it should close quickly.

Before going home, Rocky rode over to the Avon theatre and bought a ticket to the latest Elvis movie. Sitting alone, he had trouble keeping his mind focused on the screen. Halfway through the movie, he slipped out and went home.

****

Seeing her daughter lying in a coma had been heart-wrenching for Dovie Albertson, but the fact that Lilah was at peace and not in pain during the ordeal had been a blessing. Coot called Dovie, requesting that she return to the clinic, due to a new development.

When Dovie entered her daughter's room, she discovered that Lilah had awakened in a strange new world. Coot called it amnesia. He said she hadn't stopped crying and pleading for answers. He'd hoped that seeing her mother would help her regain her memory.

Dovie would never have believed the day could've come when her own daughter wouldn't recognize her. Lilah clammed up, as if she were ashamed to admit that she had no knowledge of who she was or whom she should trust.

After discussing the situation with Coot, Dovie convinced him it was best that no one know of the new development. Not yet. If word got out, Rocky would show up and cause trouble. Then with her forefinger planted against her cheek, she said, "I just had an idea." Not wanting her daughter to hear the conversation, Dovie quietly motioned for the doctor to follow her into the hall.

"Perhaps this sounds a bit far-fletched, and please don't mind calling it crazy if you feel so inclined." Then smirking, she waved it off with her hand. "Never mind. It's a silly idea."

"Hey, don't be afraid to say whatever is on your mind. I'm listening. Frankly, I'm at a loss as to what to do next. Now that she's awake, I can't keep her at the clinic indefinitely, yet I'm nervous about sending her home in her state of mind. I'm afraid of what she might do."

Dovie smiled. "My thoughts exactly. Coot, I want my daughter well. She's willing to accept that you're her doctor, but she appears hostile toward me. She resents it when I tell her I'm her mother. Do you know how that breaks my heart?"

Coot reached in his pocket and handed her a handkerchief. "She's come a long way, Big Mama, but she's confused. Give her time. I truly believe she'll gain her memory back. Now what about that idea of yours?"

"Well, it crossed my mind that if you took her into your home for a while, where you could keep watch on her until she has time to adapt, then . . . forgive me, it's a crazy idea, and probably not ethical."

He rubbed his chin, then smiled. "Why, Big Mama, I think it's a great idea, and there's nothing unethical about it. After all, Lilah is in my house at the medical center. I can transfer her to my other house on Culpepper Hill. It could serve as a half-way house, giving her time to adjust."

"Oh, then you agree?"

"Not only do I agree, as Lilah's doctor, I order it. I should've thought of it before now. Having her in my home, I'll be able to gauge her progress, and it'll be much better for her than a hospital setting."

"Exactly what I was thinking."

"I have a very compassionate housekeeper who can take care of Lilah's needs during the day. Let's do it, but we need to make sure we're both on the same page when it comes to deciding what's best for the patient."

"I fully trust you with my daughter's health, Coot. Just tell me what to do." Dovie found it difficult to hide her glee. The plan was pure genius. By the time Lilah's memory returned, as Coot anticipated, Dovie was confident her daughter would be in love with him, all over again. Why wouldn't she? He was quite the catch.

Coot said, "There's just one caveat. I hesitate to mention it, but I suppose I should. Even though you and I know this transfer is to help the patient heal, it would be best not to reveal that she has been confined to my home."

"Of course. No one has to know."

"Thank you. Now, as her caretakers, there are a few things

you and I need to discuss. Lilah is asking questions, and under no circumstances are we to lie, or argue with her. In trying to piece her life together, she'll likely come up with false assumptions. Go along. If she thinks she's the Queen of England, don't argue. It will only add to her frustration. Listen, and let her figure it out."

 He explained that even a wrong assumption could be a positive. It would mean Lilah was attempting to put things together in her head, and to attempt to change her mind would be counter-productive. He explained amnesia was like a puzzle. He said, "The fastest way to put a puzzle together is to try different pieces. You don't throw away a piece, just because it doesn't fit. The wrong piece can often lead you to recognizing the right piece."

Dovie acknowledged that she understood.

Coot suggested she go home, get all of Lilah's things and take them to his house. "Explain to the housekeeper that your daughter has been ill, and that you'll be putting her things away, since she'll be coming home with me. No other explanation is needed."

"What if she asks?"

"I think I know Ingrid well enough to know she won't ask, but if it should happen, you might explain her illness has been very difficult for you, and that you'd rather not discuss it. That would be truthful, would it not?"

She shrugged. "I can do that."

"Excellent. Why not place one of Lilah's favorite books on the bedside table and spread her cosmetics out on the dressing table? Make it feel like home to her. She'd like that, don't you think?"

"Naturally."

"Lilah and I should be home in a couple of hours. There's no need for you to be there when I we arrive. But feel free to visit your daughter in my home at any time in the future."

"I understand. I'll run by the house to grab Lilah's things and let my granddaughter know something."

Coot's brow formed a vee. "I didn't stop to think about the girl. Maybe this isn't such a wise idea."

"Oh, I don't plan to reveal her mother's whereabouts, but Cherie has to be told something, since we don't want her coming to the clinic asking questions."

"I don't know, Big Mama. This makes me nervous."

She smiled, hearing him refer to her as Big Mama. "Trust me, Coot. I can handle Cherub."

Dovie arrived home and hurriedly gathered up Lilah's things. Then walking to Cherie's door, she said, "I'll be gone for a bit, sugar. If you're hungry before I get back, there's bologna and cheese in the refrigerator. Make yourself a sandwich."

"I'm not hungry. Where are you going, and what are doing with Mama's clothes?"

"I have arrangements to make, but it shouldn't concern you. I won't be gone long. If you get bored, I sprinkled some clothes down and put them in the Frigidaire. You might iron a few."

"Arrangements? What kind of arrangements?"

"Don't ask questions, sugar. I shouldn't have said anything. The less you know, the better off you'll be. I need to go." Dovie hobbled out the door with the suitcase.

Cherie didn't get her questions answered, but she knew enough to know her mother would not need a suitcase full of clothes at the hospital.

****

Dovie drove down the long concrete driveway leading to the doctor's beautiful home, while admiring the sprawling, immaculate yards. Recalling her visit to Bellingrath Gardens last Spring with the Quarterly Meeting Group, she'd never seen anything to rival it until now. If Lilah hadn't run off with that low-life, Rocky Stone, this could've all been hers. Maybe it still could.

She hobbled up to the door. Her leg was killing her. As soon as Lilah got settled, she'd be able to stay home and keep that leg wrapped and propped up, as the doctor ordered.

She sucked in a heavy breath before knocking. This seemed like a great idea when she came up with it—but now, she wasn't so sure. Coot said they wouldn't lie, and she had agreed. But how in the Sam Hill did he think they could pull this off if they didn't bend the truth?

When the maid came to the door, Dovie said, "You must be Ingrid."

"Yes ma'am. The doctor called to let me know you were coming. Follow me, and I'll show you to Madam's room."

Dovie's pulse raced, hearing her daughter referred to as

"Madam." It sounded almost regal. She glanced around the large, beautiful room. Admittedly, there were a few loose ends that Dovie hadn't considered, but with Coot's cooperation, they'd figure it out together.

She finished putting away Lilah's belongings, then stood back and admired her creativity. The room now smacked of a feminine touch.

Returning to the clinic, she caught the doctor in the hall. Motioning for him to follow her into his office, she found it difficult to hide her enthusiasm. She told him of finding an old 8x10 picture of him and Lilah, made years ago at the Homecoming Dance. "I've kept it through the years. I framed it and placed it on the mantle in your room."

He smiled. "Ah, that night holds bittersweet memories."

"Are you saying I should remove it?"

"Not at all. It'll add the perfect touch. Lilah's memory needs jogging, and what better way than to add a photo of a memorable occasion?"

Dovie went home filled with a sense of peace that she hadn't experienced for a very long time. Not only was her daughter alive, but she was awake and would soon be in the loving arms of Dr. Sebastian Culpepper.

Coot walked into Lilah's room. "Let's go home, darling."

"Home? You? And Me? I don't understand."

He pretended not to notice the stunned look on her face, nor did he attempt an explanation. It was imperative that he allow Lilah to find her own missing pieces, regardless of how many times it took for her to shift things into the proper place. He wouldn't lie to her, but she was free to form her own conclusions. How could that wrong? He put her in a wheelchair and pushed her up to the back door of the clinic.

The nurse walked up. "I know Mrs. Stone is happy to be going home."

He said, "Nurse, would you please call and check on Mr. Thomas?"

"He's doing great. I checked last night after he got home."

"Well check again."

"Yessir."

Coot helped Lilah into his car. She said, "Who is Mrs. Tone?"

"She was a patient at the clinic."

The answer seemed to suffice. He smiled, seeing her eyes bulge when he drove up to the house.

She mumbled. "It's lovely, but I don't remember." Tears began to fall. "Oh, Coot, I don't remember this house, my likes, my dislikes . . . I don't even remember us."

"You don't have to remember, darling. Let each moment take care of itself. Be patient. These things take time." He lifted her out of the car and carried her into the house. The lump in his throat felt as if he'd swallowed a frog. Carrying Lilah across a threshold had been a lifelong dream.

He took her into the bedroom and helped her out of her robe and slippers.

"Why do I have to go to bed?"

"Your body as well as your mind has gone through a tremendous shock. I want you to rest in body, mind and spirit. Trust me, darling."

****

Cherie picked up the phone and disguising her voice, called the clinic. When the receptionist answered, she said, "Could you tell me if Mrs. Rocky Stone can have flowers delivered to her room?"

"Mrs. Stone is no longer a patient here."

Cherie tried to keep her voice from trembling. "Is she . . . is she dead?"

"I'm sorry, I'm not allowed to give out information."

Cherie hung up. So, her mother was not there, but where was she? She wanted to believe her grandmother was bringing her mother home and chose to surprise her, but if she were coming home, she wouldn't need all of her clothes. But neither would she have a need for them if she had died. None of the scenarios she came up with made sense. Unless— She picked up the phone to call her daddy. If he had been notified, he'd tell her the truth.

CHAPTER 9

Quickly unlocking the door to his hotel room, Rocky raced to pick up the ringing telephone.

"Daddy, I've been trying to call you for two hours. Where were you?"

"Hi, angel face. Why are you whispering?"

"It's Mama."

"Your mama? Is she awake? Tell me, angel. What about her?" His words all ran together.

Sobbing uncontrollably, her next words were too difficult to understand.

"Slow down and take a deep breath, sweetheart. I'm sure everything is fine. In fact, I'll go see for myself and I'll call you when I get back."

"No. No, Daddy, you don't understand."

"If you're worried about Dr. Culpepper keeping me away, that won't happen. I'll be at the clinic in ten minutes. I promise to let you know what's going on."

She screamed. "You can't see her. You aren't listening. Daddy, she's—"

"Of course I can see her. He can't stop me. She's my wife."

She screamed, "Stop it. I'm saying you can't see her because Mama isn't . . . she isn't there. Mama is not there."

Rocky took a deep breath. "Not there? What do you mean? Where is she?" His stomach wrenched. "Cherie, are you at the hospital?"

"No, sir. I'm at the farmhouse with Big Mama. She doesn't know I'm calling you. She'll be so mad if she finds out I told you. I've gotta hang up. I hear her coming."

"Wait!" But it was too late.

Rocky tried to determine what his daughter attempted to tell him in between the sobs. What did she mean when she said her mama was not there? It made no sense. Was Cherub referring to her mother's mental state? Maybe it was his fault for telling Cherie to talk to Lilah. Did it frustrate her when her mother couldn't respond? He tried to remember his daughter's exact words. Did she say, "Mama is not there . . . or she's not all there?" It was the only thing that made sense.

Hearing her cry left him brokenhearted. Rocky knew firsthand the enormous stress of living with that confounded grandmother of hers. The pressure had finally gotten to Cherub. He'd pick her up later in the evening and take her out to dinner. He'd carry her to that new restaurant across the river, but he supposed she needed time with a parent, more than she needed a thick steak. He could give her that.

First, he had to go see Lilah. Maybe she wasn't 'all there,' as Cherub indicated, but he still wanted to give her the good news about the money received from the sale of the bungalow, and the contract on the horse farm. The news was too good to keep bottled inside him. Besides, what if Coot was wrong, and she was aware of everything going on around her, but simply couldn't speak? He wanted to believe it was possible. And if it were possible, wouldn't it be wrong not to give her something to live for?

****

Cherub removed her hand from the phone and looked up to see her grandmother standing in the doorway, staring down at her.

"Who was that on the phone, shug?"

"Nobody, Big Mama."

"Nobody? Cherub, you've never lied to me, before. Why would you think it's a good time to start?"

Her lip quivered. "Because I know how much you hate him."

Dovie waddled over and plopped down in a rocker. "Come her, sweetheart, and sit in Big Mama's lap like you use to when you were a little girl."

Smiling through the tears, she said, "I'm too big to fit in your lap."

"Horsefeathers. You'll never get too big." She straightened out her dress and patted the top of her legs. "Looky what a fine lap, just the right size to hold my sweet granddaughter. Why do you think I grew such a nice big lap?"

"Maybe to hold two babies?"

"Fiddle-faddle. You're the only grandbaby I ever wanted or ever will want. I could never love another child the way I love you."

No doubt about it, it was quite a lap. Cherub walked over and sat down, laying her head on her grandmother's shoulder and bawled.

"Now, about that phone call, sugar. It was your daddy, wasn't it"

"Yes'm. I'm sorry, Big Mama."

"What did you tell him?"

"Not much. I heard you coming, and I knew you'd be mad, so I hung up."

"What does 'not much,' mean? How much?"

"I told him Mama wasn't at the hospital."

"Did he ask where she was?"

"He didn't have time. When he told me he was going to the hospital to see her, I told him not to go because she was not there, and that's when you walked in."

"I see."

"I don't see, Big Mama. If my mother was well enough to leave the hospital, why isn't she here with us?"

"It's complicated, sweet pea. You have to trust me that

everything that can be done for your mama is being done."

"Is she still in a coma?"

"Cherub, there are some things you're better off not knowing."

She jumped up. "She's dead, isn't she? You just don't want to say it. Big Mama, you said you don't want me to lie to you—well, you're lying to me, and I know it: My daddy still loves my mama, and it's not right to keep things from him."

Dovie's lips pressed together in a straight white line. Cherub knew she'd gone too far, but still she was glad she said it.

"Girlie, I won't have you speaking to me in such a disrespectful manner. You might have gotten by it with your mother, but as long as you're under my roof, I won't put up with your sass. And another thing . . . I won't have you speaking to, or about Rockwell Stone in my house. That man has no place in my life or yours. Go to your room until you can calm down."

Cherie was glad to leave the room. She didn't belong in that house. She didn't belong anywhere. Suddenly, she could understand how her mother must've felt when she decided to end it all.

****

Rocky hurried down the hall of the medical clinic, in time to see the doctor walking down the stairs. He was surprised when Coot made no effort to stop him. But it would take someone bigger than Coot Culpepper today to keep him away from his wife. He rushed into Lilah's room, then stopped short, seeing an elderly woman occupying her bed. Cherie's words now took on a new meaning.

She was right. Lilah was not there. He ran out and caught the doctor by the shirt collar. "Where is she? Where is Lilah?"

Coot reached up and removed his hand. "Calm down, Rocky. We have a couple new patients who came in this morning, and I'll thank you for lowering your voice. If you're inquiring about a former patient, I'm sorry, but I'm forbidden to relay confidential information."

"A former patient? What do you mean, *former* patient? Where's my wife, Coot? She was in no condition to leave the clinic."

The doctor's eyes squinted. "I'm sorry, Rocky, but she's gone."

Rocky paced back and forth, crying. "No. No, it can't be true. When? Why wasn't I notified?"

"Her mother handled everything. Go home, Rocky. It's over."

"Not by a long shot. Dovie didn't let me know, but it was your place to contact me, Coot."

"I understand you're upset, but I had no obligation to report to you on a patient of mine. Where were you when her mother had her admitted? Let me remind you that if you'd been living with your wife, giving her the love and affection she deserved, she wouldn't have wanted to end her life."

Rocky felt as if he'd been punched in the gut. "That's not fair. You have no idea what transpired between Lilah and me. I should've been notified."

"Rocky, if you have a problem with the decisions that were made, I'd suggest you take it up with Lilah's mother. But be gentle. The precious lady is in poor health, and she's been through a lot. She's hurting, terribly."

"Precious? Surely, we aren't talking about the same conniving ol' hag." Rocky turned, stomped down the hall and slammed the door behind him. He got in his car, laid his head on the steering wheel and wept like a baby. *Why didn't they tell me?*

Anger mixed with heartbreak caused his emotions to rock back and forth like a ship on a raging sea. *Why, Lord? Why my Lilah?* Was God punishing him? It was then he recalled the day he said, "I wish ol' lady Albertson was dead." Was this his punishment for having such a wicked thought? But he didn't mean it. Not literally. Did he? Maybe he did at the time. He couldn't say for sure. But why should Lilah have to die for his transgression? It wasn't fair. Why wouldn't God have taken him? It was his sin, not sweet Lilah's.

He drove back to the hotel and sat on the edge of the bed, trying to absorb the shocking news. He had prayed so hard for God to allow Lilah to live. *Why, Lord? Why?* He'd dreamed of telling her about the horse farm and his vision of starting over. Just the three of them. But without her, the farm meant nothing. He picked up the phone, called the realtor and told her he had to withdraw his offer. Without his family, he had no need to close the deal.

"Mr. Stone, you do realize you will lose your deposit?"

"Deposit?" He wasn't sure why the words irritated him.

"Woman, I've lost much more than that deposit. It means nothing to me." He hung up the phone, packed his belongings and checked out of the Osceola Hotel. He had to get away. But how far could he go to escape the pain?

After driving for hours with no destination in mind, Rocky was exhausted. Seeing a neon sign blinking up ahead, he whipped up in front of a dinky little motel. It wasn't much to look at, but the vacancy sign was a welcome relief. His tense shoulders ached, and his head pounded from going over all the things he should've done. . . would've done. . . could've done. But all the coulda, woulda, shoulda's didn't change a thing except to give him a splitting headache. He got out, stretched, and walked up to the Registrar's desk. "Where am I?"

"You're on the road to Kennesaw. 'Zat where you're headed?"

"If that's the road I'm on, I must be headed there."

The night manager was an older gentleman full of talk. Rocky didn't want to appear rude, but neither did he feel like carrying on a lengthy conversation with a complete stranger. He had no doubt the man's grandkids were amazing, but didn't every kid in first grade get all 'S's on their report card? After feigning a couple of wide yawns, he supposed he'd gotten his point across when the old fellow pulled a key from a cubby hole and shoved toward him.

"Room 104. You can drive your car around to the back. It's the one on the corner. Check-out is twelve o'clock noon."

Rocky nodded. He realized he'd offended the man, but he'd try to make it up to him in the morning when it would be easier to pretend interest in a stranger's family history.

The motel room was small and sparsely furnished, but it had all the essentials: a bed and a bathroom. The mattress was lumpy, and he'd encountered church pews which were more conducive to sleep, but at least he could stretch out.

He tossed and turned all night, but sleep wouldn't come. The words he wish he'd said to Lilah rolled around in his head. But it wasn't the words which he failed to say that haunted him as much as the unfair ultimatum he gave her.

She loved him. He knew it. And he loved her. But he forced her to make a difficult choice between two people she loved dearly.

They spoke words in haste that neither of them meant. She had too much pride to ask him to come home, and he had too much pride to go back. Both were stubborn, yet neither could bear the thought of living without the other. Rocky pulled a pillow over his head, as if he could smother the recurring dark thoughts of joining her. His aching heart told him he had no choice. He had to go on living. They had a daughter who needed him.

He should've gone to see Cherub before leaving town. He could only imagine how distraught she must be. But how much help could he have been in his state of mind? He had to get his own emotions under control before attempting to comfort his sweet girl.

CHAPTER 10

The following morning, Rocky drove until he saw a sign, saying, *Welcome to Kennesaw, Georgia.* He'd heard of Kennesaw Mountain, but it was the first time he'd seen it.

Not far from the mountain was a local eating joint and judging from all the cars in the parking lot, he assumed it would be a good place to eat. Didn't folks cook their own breakfast anymore? But after ordering, he understood. The food was good, the prices decent, but it wasn't simply a place to eat. It was obviously a gathering place for the locals to catch up on the latest news.

The waitress was exceptionally friendly, and everyone in the room appeared to love her the way they carried on foolishness with her. The jovial atmosphere helped to lighten his heavy heart.

The waitress walked up to him, clicked her tongue the way one does when prompting a horse to take off, and said, "Hey, good-looking. Haven't seen you around these parts, What handle do you go by?"

"Rocky. Rocky Stone."

Tossing her long hair back with a quick jerk of her head, she laughed. "I'd say that's gonna be a hard name to remember. Very hard."

"Save your jokes. You won't come up with anything I haven't heard before."

"Nice to meet you, Rocky Stone. I'm Sandy Beach."

His lip curled. "Hi, Sandy." She laughed. "Seriously. Your name is Rocky Stone?"

"Yep!"

"Well, I love it. It sounds like a name for a movie star. Say, you do look familiar. You aren't—"

"A movie star? Not me, Pilgrim."

"Good try, but I didn't mistake you for John Wayne. So, you're Rocky! Ever been called Rock?"

"I've been called a lot of things."

She pinched her chin and appeared to be mulling over the name. "Are you sure your last name is Stone and not Hudson?"

"Do I get a discount if it is?"

She laughed. "I like you, Rocky Stone. My name is Rebecca, but folks around here call me Becky." He loved hearing her laugh. It made him feel as if he were in friendly territory—a feeling he hadn't had in a while.

Rocky picked up the menu from off the table, but she grabbed it back. "You'll want the two eggs, grits, bacon and pancakes."

"I will?"

"Sure. It's better to get the special. Cheaper that way. Eat what you want and leave the rest. How you like your eggs and bacon?"

"Uh—eggs over medium with crispy bacon."

"Got it."

He found the people in the cafe to be exceptionally cordial to the new face in town. Before he finished his pancakes, he'd become acquainted with half the folks in the dining room. When the waitress questioned his destination, he shrugged. "The jury is still out. Any suggestions of a good place to hang my hat?"

"Sure. Kennesaw."

He laughed. "Here?"

"Why not here?"

"Uh . . . I was only kidding when I asked for suggestions—"

"Sorry. I thought you were serious. So where are you going, or is it rude of me to ask?"

"I don't mind you asking. It's just that I don't have an answer."

"What line of work are you in?"

The girl was full of questions, but he didn't find it offensive. It was obvious she was attempting to be friendly. "I started out hog farming, but I've also worked in a chenille mill. I recently considered ranching, and I think I might've liked it. Who knows? Maybe I'll give it a try later. Honestly, I have no idea what comes next. I recently lost my wife."

Her face blushed. "I'm sorry. I shouldn't have been so nosey.

It's become a bad habit of mine."

"No problem. To be truthful, I have no idea what I want to do or where I want to go next. Whatever I decide will have to be somewhere I feel is a good place to raise my little girl."

"So, you have a kid. How old is she?" She put her hand over her mouth." There I go again, asking too many personal questions."

"Almost sixteen."

"Gracious! She's not a little girl. Man, she's 'nearbout' grown. At sixteen, you won't have her around long. Some fellow will come along and sweep her right out from under your feet. But if you're serious about relocating, you won't find a better place than right here in Kennesaw, Georgia. We've got hog farmers, cattle farmers, dirt farmers, storekeepers and ranchers, and if you have a hankering to try another field, you'll not find a friendlier place to get a new start."

Three men sitting at a table across from him, echoed her words. One said, "Have you had experience working on cars? I could use a paint and body man." Another suggested he might contact Max about working for him at the grocery store. The third said, "If he's a hog farmer, he ain't gonna be satisfied with an indoor job. Am I right, Mr. Rocky Stone?"

Rocky smiled. He stood and left a tip on the table. "You're probably right." Then tipping his cap, he said, "It's been a pleasure meeting you folks." Before cranking his car to leave, he found himself asking the same question Becky had asked. "Why not Kennesaw?" It was a good question, since he had too many sad memories in Nearby and no other destination in mind.

The remainder of the afternoon was spent riding around the little town, looking for a place to rent. After going down every street in town, he pulled up to a service station. He bought five dollars' worth of Ethyl, had his oil checked, and windshield cleaned. The attendant stuck the chamois cloth in his hip pocket. "Where you headed, if you don't mind me asking?"

Rocky explained he was toying with the idea of moving to Kennesaw or at least somewhere in the vicinity. "Would you happen to know of a house for rent?"

The fellow took off his cap, ran his hands through greasy hair, then slowly shook his head. "Can't rightly say that I do." His eyes suddenly lit up. "Can't think of nothin' to rent, right off the bat, but Granny Knox's young'uns just put her in the old folks home. Hear tell they plan on selling her place, but I don't reckon that would interest you."

"I'd rather rent a place first to see if I'm gonna like it here."

The man laughed as if he'd heard a joke. "If that's all that holds you back, I'd say drive over there and check it out while Granny's young'uns are still in town. You'll like living here. That's a given. Course now, the place is probably a bit pricey. It's an old house, but well-built and big enough to raise a family in. I suppose you've got family?"

Rocky bit his lip to stop the trembling. "Yes. Yes, I do. I have a teenage daughter."

The man scratched his head. "No wife?"

"I'm a widower." A lump formed in his throat. It was the first time he'd said it, and it hurt.

"That's a shame. I lost my wife too. Back in thirty-nine. Don't reckon I'll ever get over losing her."

Wanting to end the painful conversation, Rocky pulled a notepad and pencil from his shirt pocket. "Could you write down the address of the house?"

"Shucks. Don't need to write it down." He stepped toward the road and pointed. "Go straight down this road until you come to the crossroads. Take a right and when you see a grocery store on your left, you'll take another right. The store has gas pumps out front, but it's been closed ever since Dudley died, and I reckon that's been ten years ago. I take that back. It's been longer than that, because my little granddaughter Sara started school that year. The reason I remember is because—" He threw up his hand. "Shucks, that ain't what you asked, is it? Don't reckon you had no way of knowing Dudley, but he was a fine fellow. He won the turkey shoot five years in a row. But now, that ol' lady of his was somethin' else."

Rocky grimaced. "So, after I turn right, then what?"

The old fellow appeared offended. "Go about a mile, the road veers off to the left and that's when you'll see it. It's a sprawling big house. Probably too big for just you and the girl, but it's the only place I can think of that might be available. Most of the folks in Kennesaw were born and raised here, and those who weren't are in no hurry to leave. We like it here."

Attempting to make up for his lack of patience, Rocky reached out his hand. "I'm much obliged for your willingness to help, and I can understand why no one wants to leave." It worked.

The man gripped his hand and smiled. "Well, I hope things work out for you, son. We'd be happy to have you and your daughter living amongst us."

Rocky was confident he wouldn't remember the directions the fellow at the service station gave, but what difference did it make? He had no serious thoughts of buying a house. He planned to rent a place until he knew where he needed to be, and it wouldn't be in Kennesaw. This was merely a way-station until he could decide what to do. But what better place to figure it out?

He felt an ache in the pit of his stomach. In times past, when he and Lilah faced a big decision, they prayed and asked God for direction. But he had prayed for Lilah to live and to take him back . . . but it didn't happen. Why did some people have all their prayers answered, while his bounced off the walls? It wasn't fair.

He could hear his sweet wife's voice in his head saying, "God is good, Rocky, even when life isn't fair." His life became excruciatingly unfair the day he demanded Lilah choose between him and her mother. When she couldn't live with her decision, what did she do? She ingested poison and left him bearing all the pain. The tears flowed down Rocky's face like an uncapped well. He whipped over to the side of the road, bowed his head and prayed. "Dear God—" But that was as far as he got. His throat tightened. Rocky could remember times when he felt so close to the Lord, he could pray in his closet for over an hour at the time, but that seemed so very long ago. Now, he had wandered too far away to find his way back. Did he even want to? Little good it had done him. Had he left God or had God left him?

Preacher Curtis said the Bible says we are to thank God *in* all things. He stressed that it didn't say *for* all things, but what was the difference? *In* or *for* . . . how could he be thankful that Lilah decided to swallow a toxic substance to end her life? Easy for the preacher to say. He still had his wife. Rocky beat on the steering wheel and screamed. "Why, Lilah? Why? Why did you do it? If only I had known I would've stayed. There it was again. *If only*—"

Rocky drove back to the motel and asked to rent the room for one more night. He was in no shape to drive anywhere.

The following morning, Rocky packed his bag and drove back to the little café for the breakfast special. The same folks were there, and the joy he sensed among them reminded him of the words in the twenty-third Psalm. Truly, their cups were full and running over. He remembered what it felt like, but it had been a long time. Would he ever feel that lighthearted again? It was doubtful.

The door from the kitchen to the dining room swung open, and the waitress came strolling out, holding two platters, which she put on the table in front of Max and Lloyd. Rocky felt proud of himself that he remembered their names.

Becky walked over to Rocky's table and laid her hand on his shoulder. He sucked in a lungful of air. The human touch felt good. He wasn't sure why. There was nothing sexual in it, but rather a soothing, comforting feeling, as if she understood what he was going through. Yet, there was no way. No one could possibly understand.

"What can I get for you, Cowboy?"

He feigned a smile. "How about that same special I had yesterday?"

"Coming up."

Max and Lloyd acknowledged his presence and included him in their camaraderie, although he hadn't felt much like joining in the conversation. Becky came back with his meal, then pulled out a chair and sat down.

She said, "I only have a minute, but I wanted to tell you that Sam is selling the joint if you're interested. He lives in the garage apartment back of the café, so it'll be a package deal. Sadie died over three years ago, and his kids want him to move to Eufaula so they can help care for him."

Rocky chuckled at the ridiculous notion of him running a café, but even funnier was the fact that she would've thought he could be interested. "Thanks, but I know nothing about food preparation or restaurant management, and frankly the idea terrifies me."

"You could do it. I've been running the place for years. Until he had the stroke, Sam showed up every morning, but Rosalie and Willie do all the cooking, and I do the rest." She laughed. "Sam's primary job was to take the money to the bank." She jumped up. "Oops, here comes Mr. Charlie and Miz Mary. Excuse me." Then looking back at Rocky, she said, "Forget I said anything. I don't know why I felt the need to share that bit of information with you. It wasn't my place."

He thanked her, although he wondered the same thing. If he remembered correctly, all the chatter about him finding employment in Kennesaw was brought about by the folks there in the café. All he mentioned needing was a place to rent. They jumped on it and had already informed him where the voting precinct was located.

By the time he finished his breakfast, the place had almost cleared out. Becky walked over to his table and sat down with a cup of coffee. "The rush starts about six a.m., and at eleven o'clock, I lock the doors."

"So, you only serve one meal a day?"

"Yeah. We did serve dinner before Sam got laid up. He's been in the hospital over a week and to tell the truth I'll be surprised if he gets out of their alive. I'm sorry if I came across as if I were trying to push the café on you, but I can't buy it, and I can't think of anyone in Kennesaw who might be interested. But if someone doesn't step up soon, we'll have to close."

He felt for her, but not badly enough to buy a café, for goodness sake. "I'm sorry to hear that. I wish I could help."

"I understand. I'll keep praying about it. I don't know why I allow myself to think I have to work it out, when I know in my heart the Lord will provide."

Rocky pursed his lips. "How do you know?"

She looked at him as if he'd grown horns. "Because He told me."

He hadn't meant to roll his eyes and hoped she didn't notice. Slowly sipping on his second cup of coffee, he found it impossible to dismiss their conversation. He had to check out of the motel by twelve. So where would he go from here? It would've been nice if he could've found a place to rent closer to town. The friendly atmosphere had helped to get his mind on something besides the anger he felt inside.

Becky mentioned a garage apartment. Would the old man rent the apartment until he could sell the Sam & Sadie? If it would take as long to sell the café as Becky predicted, it would give Rocky time to decide what he wanted to do from here. It was worth a try. He decided with nowhere in particular to go, he'd wait around until the café was empty before approaching the subject.

When the time was right, he inquired about Sam, while trying not to sound overly interested.

"He's in Emory Hospital in Atlanta. I talked with him on the phone last night, and he doesn't want to leave Kennesaw until he finds a buyer, but his son is insisting he put a padlock on the door and move to Eufaula right away." She laughed.

"What's funny?"

"Just thinking the son is wasting his breath. Sam Toler is not one to be pushed into doing something he's not ready to do, and he doesn't want to see The Sam & Sadie close."

"What will you do if it does close?"

"Like I said, the Lord will provide."

"Oh, yeah. I forgot. He told you He would."

"Yep! And that's not all that He told me, friend. He said He's got you in the palm of His hand."

Surely, she was joking, so he chuckled, although it came out sounding fake, even to him.

CHAPTER 11

Rocky left the café and drove straight to the hospital in Atlanta. It was much larger than he had imagined. Walking from his car, the first thing he noticed was the fact that folks didn't speak as he tipped his cap and greeted them. No one even looked him in the eye. Kennesaw wasn't so far from Atlanta, yet he felt as if he'd been transported to another country. So, what was the divide? Why did he feel so welcomed by strangers in Kennesaw, but snubbed by people he passed by, only thirty miles away?

He walked up to the information desk and asked for Sam Toler's room. He thought it odd that the lady didn't have to look up the room number. After giving him directions, she said, "That fellow apparently has lots of friends. Folks have been coming and going up there as if he has a rotating door, but you've come at a good time. I believe I saw his last visitor walk out the front door only minutes ago."

Rocky approached door #402 and made a fist, prepared to

knock. All the 'what if's' that he hadn't stopped to consider, suddenly flooded his thoughts. What if Cherub hated Kennesaw? Of course, she would. She was in love. Would he have wanted to move away from Nearby when he was fifteen and so in love with the pretty young thing with golden curls and big blue eyes that melted his heart? Would he lose his daughter forever if he moved her so far away?

He turned and walked back out, faster than he walked in. He couldn't make such a drastic decision without talking with her first.

Driving down Highway 41, he couldn't get Becky out of his mind. Why wasn't a pretty young woman like her married? But then, he knew absolutely nothing about her, except she had a great personality and seemed sweet. For all he knew, she could've been married several times. A funny thought crossed his mind. She could be an axe murderer, for crying out loud. Then, chuckling to himself, he wondered if Lizzie Borden was sweet. His thoughts turned back to his daughter. Maybe she'll want to get a new start in a new town—just the two of them. Rocky ran his fingers through his hair. He'd drive back to Nearby and approach her with the idea. They'd drive over to Dothan for a nice dinner to discuss it. He'd tell her all about the friendly people in Kennesaw. She'd like Becky. Everybody liked Becky. If he bought the café, Cherie could help her wait on tables. She'd like that. Wouldn't she? Cherub was a people person, just like her mother had been. The longer he thought about it, the more convinced he was that it was a great idea. He couldn't wait to present it to her.

Looking at the speedometer, he eased up on the accelerator. The last thing his daughter needed was to lose her only other parent. She needed him. And he needed her.

****

Dovie Albertson opened the mailbox, took out three pieces of mail, and threw an envelope with a Georgia postmark into the outdoor trash can. No way would she allow Rocky Stone to mess with her granddaughter's emotions. Didn't the child have enough on her plate without having that man upset her? It was her job to protect Cherie. It's what Lilah would want.

She glanced up to see Cherie standing in the doorway.

"Big Mama? You're crying." Placing her arm around her grandmother's waist—or as far as she could reach—they walked into the house. She said, "I miss her, too. Daddy says it sometimes helps to cry. He says if tears come from the left eye first it means that—"

"Goodness gracious, child. Don't repeat the nonsense that comes from your daddy. He makes up ninety-percent of the junk he tells you. And for your information, I wasn't crying.
It's these confounded allergies, hon. Happens every year about this time. I love peanuts, but it sure messes up my sinuses when the farmers start stacking." Then shooing Cherie off with her hand, she said, "Now, stop dawdling and go clean your room."

"It's clean, Big Mama. I came looking for you to ask you

something."

"Sure, shug, but be quick about it. Your ol' Big Mama has got a thousand things to do today. What's on your mind?"

"Something that's been troubling me. Can't we sit down for just a minute to talk about it?"

Dovie's throat tightened. So many questions with so few answers swirled in her head. How much longer could she put Cherie off? Wasn't she doing the right thing by sparing her precious granddaughter the heartbreaking details? Doesn't the Bible say God won't put more on a body than one can stand? She tried to look up the verse not long after Lilah took the rat poison but finally gave up. She shrugged. So, maybe it's not in the Bible, but she heard it somewhere and it seemed it ought to be in there if it wasn't.

"Big Mama, please?"

"Hon, can't it wait?"

"No ma'am. I gotta know."

Why keep pretending Cherie would eventually stop asking. It wasn't going away. "Well, I reckon I can spare a minute or two. Sit in the swing and tell me what's in that pretty little head."

"I wanna know the truth. Did Mama die? And if she did, why wasn't there a funeral?"

Dovie's eyes welled with water and ran down her weathered face. Her lips trembled. "Cherub Helena Stone, why do you insist on making this so hard for your poor granny? You know I hate funerals."

Cherie bit her lip. Any time her grandmother called her by her whole name, she knew she'd overstepped her bounds. "I never knew that, Big Mama."

"Law, child, can't you see this is the hardest thing I've ever had to go through? I'm gonna say this once and you aren't to bring it up again. Do you understand?"

Cherub nodded.

Her voice quivered. "Good. Then listen and listen good for it's the last time we're gonna talk about it. Sugar, I know you miss her. But your mama is no longer in pain. She's gone to a beautiful place and one day we'll all be together. As comforting as that should be to us both, dwelling on it hurts me." Tears welled in her eyes. "There! I've told you the truth and I won't say it again. I like to pretend my sweet girl is going to come walking in that door at any minute. I know deep down it's not gonna happen, but I won't have you taking that beautiful vision away from me by making me dwell on the fact that she can't be with us."

"I'm sorry, Big Mama. Can we go put flowers on her grave?"

"Standing over a gravesite does no one a lick of good. It only causes more weeping, and besides, my precious Lilah Jean, is not there."

"Is Mama in heaven already? Some folks say people in heaven can see what's going on down here. Do you think she knows how much I miss her?"

"Would it really be heaven if folks up there could look down and see their loved ones grieving and all the turmoil that's taking place, here on earth?"

"I reckon not. I hadn't thought about it like that."

Big Mama glanced at her watch and stood. "I've sat here longer than I aimed to. If you have nothing else to do, child, how about running the Stanley dust mop over the floors? It's amazing how much dust accumulates in this old house." The old woman wiped her eyes with the tale of her apron.

Cherie wrapped her grandmother in her arms. "I'm sorry Big Mama. I promise not to pester you anymore. Please don't cry. I miss her, too."

"Law, shug, I know you do. But we'll get through this, together."

"Yes'm, we will Big Mama, but there's one more thing that worries me."

"Save it. We've wasted enough time."

"Yes ma'am." Cherie stood. "I was just gonna say I haven't heard from my daddy. I'm afraid something has happened to him. I called the Osceola Hotel and was told he left. It's not like him to disappear without a word."

"Bless your heart, sugar, that's really what's troubling you, isn't it? And I can see how it would. I reckon I've been wrong to shield you, but I can't cover for Rocky Stone forever. Sit back down. I reckon this is more important than getting the clothes hung on the line. It's time you face the fact that if your daddy cared about anyone other than himself, he would've been here for you. He chose to wash his hands of you and Lilah months ago. I think the only reason he hung around as long as he did was because he was waiting for me to die, thinking he'd get the farmhouse and two-hundred acres of the best farmland around. But this place goes to you when I die, and the only thing I ask of you is that you never let that man move in and take over. I don't want him to have any part of it."

"Big Mama, do you really hate him that much?"

"Hate? Shame on you. You know I don't hate nobody. That ain't Christian. I just don't plan to reward Rocky after the way he's treated you and my daughter. He knows you're hurting, but does he care?"

The lump in her throat swelled. "I don't know."

"Well, I do, and sadly the answer is 'not one whit. If it wasn't for that man, Lilah Jean would be here with us today. He lied to her so many times, I don't know how she took it as long as she did. He might as well have poured the bottle of poison down her throat, since he's the one who drove her to it.'"

Her grandmother's blunt words cut to the bone. Cherie thought nothing could be as terrible as losing her mother but facing the truth that her daddy didn't love her was every bit as painful, but in a different way. Perhaps she should be angry with her mother for leaving her, but somehow she'd been able to forgive her. But Big Mama was right. He didn't deserve forgiveness for abandoning her when she needed him most.

There was so much more Cherie wanted to know—so many unanswered questions—but she'd made her grandmother a promise she couldn't break. Big Mama had always seemed so strong, but losing her only daughter had definitely taken a toll on her.

CHAPTER 12

Rocky Stone was on the road again, headed back to Kennesaw. Driving through Atlanta, he stopped at Emory Hospital and took the elevator up to Room 402. A man in his forties opened the door.

Rocky introduced himself and discovered the fellow was Mr. Toler's son. He seemed delighted to hear that Rocky could possibly be interested in purchasing The Sam & Sadie.

"You're a Godsend. I suppose Becky told you we need to sell?"

Rocky nodded.

"She's been running the place for years, and I hope if you do decide to purchase, you'll continue to keep her. She's very dependable and all the folks love her. She's there to open up every morning and sees to it that everything runs smoothly."

Rocky chuckled. "You don't have to sell her to me. I have absolutely no restaurant experience, and I wouldn't consider purchasing it without her agreeing to manage it for me."

"Years ago, when Mama and Dad were much younger, they kept it open for three meals a day. After Mama got sick, they started closing after lunch around two o'clock. But after Dad's health declined, it's only been open for breakfast. Just saying, you'll have the support of the town, regardless of the hours you choose to stay open."

"I think I'd rather stay with breakfast only until I learn what I'm doing."

"Sounds logical. I suppose you're aware that the garage apartment comes furnished? Dad won't be needing it. If it's not to your taste, there's a fellow who eats in the cafe every morning named Tony. He has a truck and would be happy to take any of it off your hands."

"Thanks, I've met Tony, but the furniture is a plus. My plans are to move in immediately and in time I'll be bringing my sixteen-year-old daughter to live with me." He was glad the man didn't question him about a wife. He wasn't ready to talk about it.

"Sixteen?"

Rocky nodded. Well, she will be in a couple of days. I just got back from taking her birthday present to her." He almost wished he hadn't brought it up, since he didn't want to go into the agonizing details of why Cherub wasn't with him.

But the guy didn't question it. "I guess Becky told you she has a younger sister, who is away at school?"

He shook his head. "No, I didn't know, but then our

conversations have centered around the café and not our personal lives."

"I understand. Well, you'll love the kid. She's a sweetheart. Stays in Kennesaw with Becky every summer and helps out. The customers love her. How long have you been in the restaurant business?"

Rocky grinned. "Let's see . . . tomorrow is Tuesday. Right?"

"That's right."

"Well, if we could close the deal in the morning, then ask me again Wednesday, because by then it will have been twenty-four hours."

The man laughed out loud. "You're kidding."

"Nope. You're thinking I'm crazy, I know."

"Not at all. As long as you have Becky running the place, it'll be the easiest job you've ever had. She's swell."

The part about "as long as you have Becky," didn't get past him. His stomach suddenly felt as if he'd swallowed Mexican jumping beans. What assurance did he have that she wouldn't leave? He tried to concentrate on the conversation at hand. "I'm sorry. You were saying?"

He was glad the man wasn't offended. "I said Mama and Daddy built the cafe over forty years ago and the garage apartment in the back was home to me growing up. Mama died three years ago and now that Dad has had a stroke, he won't be able to climb the stairs."

From the looks of the frail old man, Rocky could understand.

He wasn't sure Sam would make it out of the hospital. A reasonable price was quickly agreed upon and Rocky would've given more had they asked. The son had Power of Attorney, and before nightfall, the proper documents were signed, and all parties left the table feeling the deal was a good one.

Rocky Stone was now the proud owner of a restaurant, a two-bedroom garage apartment, money in the bank, but with a huge empty hole in his heart. What good was any of it without the ones he loved? He trudged up the stairs of the apartment, fell across the bed and cried. "Delilah, baby, why? Why did you do it?" How many times had he asked this same question? Did he really have to ask why, when he knew the answer? The stupid ultimatum. "I'm so sorry, baby. I can't live without you." The words coming from his lips stunned him, but it only took a minute to know it was true. What did he have to live for?

His pulse raced as he contemplated ending the pain. "Hold on, sweetheart, I'm coming." The thought of ending the pain gave him a peculiar feeling of euphoria. He opened his duffel bag and jerked everything out, tossing it on the floor, before remembering his pistol was under the front seat of the car.

Halfway down the stairs, he heard a voice say, "Stop!" Rocky stopped short and looked down at the bottom of the stairs, then turned his head and looked up. His heart raced. *The voice sounded— that's impossible.* He shrugged it off and hurried to his car. Reaching under the seat he felt the cold steel. Then came the voice again. "Rocky, stop."

This time, it called him by name. Sweat popped out on his brow. "Lilah? Lilah, can you hear me?" Crazy thoughts swirled in his head. *Lilah is dead and I don't believe in ghosts. The stress is causing me to lose my mind.* Wasn't that even more reason to end his life? Rocky withdrew his hand from under the seat, holding tightly to the pistol. He offered up a quick prayer of explanation to God, informing Him why He should understand that life had become too difficult to handle. He lifted his arm, with the barrel of the gun pressed against his temple. His hand shook when his finger touched the trigger.

"STOP!" Once again, the voice was as clear as if someone were sitting beside him. Not someone. But Lilah. In his heart, he knew it wasn't his wife. Impossible. The voice was in his head. Had to be. Beginning to hyperventilate, he quickly shoved the gun back under the seat, convincing himself he wasn't thinking clearly and should wait until he was confident that he knew exactly what he was doing. He trudged back up the stairs to the apartment, fell across the bed and cried himself to sleep.

Rocky awakened the next morning confused. Then it all came back. His wife was dead, and his daughter hated him. He chewed the inside of his jaw as he relived putting the pistol to his head. He remembered the eerie feeling he had when he placed his finger on the trigger, ready to pull.

Yet here he was, alive and well, all because of an imaginary, yet very real sounding voice in his head demanding that he stop. Common sense told him that even though it sounded exactly like Lilah's voice, that it couldn't have been since it's impossible to hear from the dead. *God?* Could it be? He shrugged at the absurdity of the passing thought. He and God weren't on the best of terms. The only explanation he came up with for the strange phenomenon was that his own conscience had cried out to prevent him from making a drastic mistake.

How dreadful it would've been if he'd carried out his plan. He had a daughter and therefore had a really good reason to stick around. Even though she was angry with him, he wasn't ready to give up on her. She needed him, even though she didn't realize it yet.

He dressed, then trekked over to the café. When he walked inside, the applause took him by surprise. He looked at Becky, who stood holding a platter and grinning.

The room was filled. Rocky looked around. "What's going on?"

Becky said, "It's our thanks, boss."

"Thanks? For what?"

Lloyd said, "We knew Sam couldn't keep the place open and some of us have been having breakfast here for thirty years or longer. The thought of it closing was most distressing."

Tony said, "True. Every important occasion in our lives is

celebrated at the Sam & Sadie. For it to close would've been like losing a part of us. I don't know if Becky told you, but we all got together almost five months ago and held a prayer meeting. We prayed for the Lord to send us someone who could keep the place going. I'm ashamed to admit I had almost given up. And then, Glory to God, He sent you here."

Max nodded in agreement. "What Tony is trying to tell you, Mr. Stone, is that we all know you aren't here by accident. You're our gift from the Lord." Max's comment drew loud 'Amen's' from around the room.

Rocky thanked them. If they chose to believe that he was in Kennesaw because God answered their prayers, what good would it do to dispute it? The only thing he knew for sure was that God certainly hadn't answered any of his prayers, lately.

Months ago, he prayed for Lilah to understand that their marriage was in peril, and the only way to save it would be for her to send her mother packing. But that didn't happen. Instead, Lilah attempted suicide. Then, he prayed for her to live. And that didn't happen. Distraught and with no direction in mind, he wound up on the road to Kennesaw. He didn't hear a voice from Heaven saying, "Ye shall abide here." Nope. He heard nothing. The only reason to stop there was because he was too tired to drive further. He couldn't explain why he felt drawn to the quaint little town, the café, and the people, but there was something about it that gave him a sense of peace, which he hadn't known for quite some time.

So, once again, he prayed. This time he prayed that he and his daughter could get a fresh new start in the little Georgia town. And that didn't happen. Cherub was quick to let him know she wanted nothing to do with him. What good did all the praying do?

Realizing every eye was focused on him, Rocky gave a short speech, thanking everyone for being so gracious. "This is all going to be new to me, so I covet your patience as I maneuver through the learning process. I've never worked in a restaurant and certainly never considered owning one. It has happened so fast, I haven't had time for it to sink in."

When he stated that as long as Becky was there to run the place, they could dispel any rumors of the café closing, it drew a second round of applause. Feeling awkward at being the center of attention, Rocky asked Becky to say a few words and he quickly took a seat at the nearest table.

Becky assured him the employees had everything under control and that his only real responsibility would be to write the checks and deposit the money. There seemed to be no reason to change things, since the café was running like a well-oiled wheel. The only change he wanted to make would be to give Becky a nice raise. He couldn't chance losing her.

CHAPTER 13

For weeks, Rocky got up every morning, walked over to the café and sat around 'chewing the fat' with the regulars. He smiled, realizing he was beginning to think like them. It hadn't taken long for the folks in Kennesaw to begin to feel like an extended family, and if there was one thing he needed in order to keep his mind off all that he'd lost, it was a sense of belonging.

If he had favorites, he'd have to say it was Miss Reba and Miss Annie. They were too old-maid sisters, and it didn't take long for them to designate themselves as his personal caretakers. At times, he could've enjoyed a little less care, but the old souls meant well, and he supposed they needed something to fill their days.

It wasn't unusual to awaken to the sounds of their voices in his kitchen, as they "tidied up," as they called it.

"Miss Annie, it's very thoughtful of you and Miss Reba to want to help, but honestly, it isn't necessary. I'm capable of taking care of myself."

The wrinkles around her eyes deepened when she squinted. She turned, winked at her sister, and in perfect harmony, they cackled, as if that were the silliest thing they'd ever heard. Miss Annie said, "Why, sugar, if we didn't have you to fuss over, what in the world would we do all day?"

Miss Reba lifted her right hand as if about to take an oath. "That's the Gospel truth. After Sadie died, Sister and I felt it our God-called duty to take care of Sam. Sadie would've wanted it, you know."

Rocky hoped his thoughts weren't written on his forehead. How could he know what Sadie would've wanted? He'd never met the woman, and his encounter with Sam with brief. The only thing he knew for sure was that leaving pants lying on the floor and dirty clothes stuffed under the bed didn't bother him half as much as having two sweet old ladies constantly walking behind him, picking up whatever he happened to leave behind. How could he get the point across without offending?

Annie interrupted. "Sister is right. Our days have been long and boring since Sam went into the hospital and when we heard he wouldn't be coming back, we felt our job on earth was done. No one needed us. It's a bad feeling not to be needed, don't you know."

That, he could confirm.

Reba put her arm around her sister's waist and smiled. "That's exactly right. A bad feeling, indeed, but lo and behold, the Lord has now given us an exciting new mission."

Rocky sucked in a lungful of air. How should he phrase it? "You are both very sweet, and it's not that I don't appreciate all you do for me, but I need to learn to do things for myself."

The way the sisters looked at one another and grinned, made him recount his last words. He was sure it hadn't come out the way he intended, for their enthusiasm was unmistakable.

Annie's mouth gaped open the way a child's does on Christmas morning, after discovering gifts under the tree. She gleefully exclaimed, "Isn't it wonderful how the Lord always provides the supply before the need? This is even better than we could've hoped for. Right, sister?"

Reba nodded.

Scratching his head, he said, "I beg your pardon?"

"Don't you get it, Sonny boy? You have expressed a desire to learn to do things for yourself, but God provided the supply even before you realized you had the need. But isn't that just like the Lord?"

"Excuse me, but you must've misunderstood what I was attempting to say."

"Oh, we understand, alright. Brother Duncan preached it last Sunday. The Lord always provides the supply before the need."

Annie said, "Sister, I'm not sure Sonny boy has embraced the message. You see, Sonny, God made the sea before he created the fish and the air before the birds. Now, do you understand?"

Understand? He was more confused than before. The longer

they stayed, the less sense they made. He'd have to say it gently yet make it plain enough for them to understand that he didn't need nor want to wake up every morning with two old women in the apartment, sweet as they were.

"I'm sorry, ladies, I'm afraid I haven't made myself clear—"

Reba said, "Oh, we know exactly what you were saying. We can begin by teaching you how to fold your trousers."

Annie smiled. "Excellent idea, Reba, dear." Then turning to Rocky, she said, "Sonny boy, if you'd like to slip them off, I can show you how to hang them so the creases will stay straight."

What? He supposed it was dementia, but he'd began to wonder who was demented. Him or the Duvall sisters?

Reba chimed in. "What Annie means is that you should hang your trousers in the closet if they aren't soiled. But if they're dirty, you'll find a hamper in the bathroom. The washing machine is in the garage. If you don't know how to operate it, we'll be glad to teach you. The ringer can be tricky. Sister got her hand caught in it after Sam first bought it."

He was glad they didn't press him to take off his pants.

Reba clasped her hands together under her chin. "Oh, sister, this is going to be such a fun mission."

Rocky rubbed his hand across the back of his neck, contemplating how he could put a stop to this without hurting the sweet old souls. Standing between them, he placed an arm around both. "Ladies, I have a confession to make."

Annie looked at Reba and frowned. "Oh, we weren't aware you were Catholic."

"I beg your pardon?"

"I don't think we have a priest in Kennesaw."

Reba said "Sister is right. You'll need to drive over to Marietta to the church in the square. But now that I'm thinking about it, that may be a Presbyterian. But I'm sure there's a Catholic church there somewhere."

"But I'm not Catholic."

"Then why do you need a priest?"

"I didn't say I needed one."

Miss Annie said, "Not meaning to dispute you, Sonny boy, but sister and I heard you say you needed to go to confession." She reached up and with the back of her hand felt his forehead. "Are you sure you're feeling all right?"

"I'm afraid you misunderstood. I said, I had a confession to make. I meant I need to confess something to both of you."

"Bless your heart, you're sweet, but we don't do confessions. When we have something weighing heavily upon us, we just tell it to Jesus."

Reba began to sing a few lines to a song, "Tell it to Jesus, tell it to Jesus, He is a friend that's well known, you have no other such a friend or brother, tell it to Jesus alone—"

Rocky interrupted. "That's lovely. But I'm afraid I'm having difficulty making myself clear. Please allow me to explain." He talked very slowly and very distinctly, not wanting a single word to get past them. "It's not that I don't know how to hang my pants or wash my clothes. When I said I need to learn to do things for myself, I didn't really mean I *had* to learn."

Annie nodded. "We understood. You meant to say you have a need to learn."

"No ma'am. That is what you heard, but what I meant to say was that I know how, but I haven't been doing a very good job, lately. I'd like to say I want to do better, but I'm not sure that would be true. Sometimes I enjoy leaving my pants lying on the floor. I know you ladies don't mind fussing over me, as you call it, and I do love you for wanting to help. But the need is not here."

The sisters glared at one another. Then Annie said, "Are you saying you don't need us?"

"Of course, I need you. But not to clean my apartment or do my laundry or hang my clothes."

"Then what can we do for you?"

"You can pray for me." The pat answer spilled out before he had time to think about what he was saying. Nevertheless, the response seemed to delight them both.

Annie pulled a notepad and pencil from her pocketbook. "Here, Sonny. Write down your requests and sister and I will pray over each one every night before retiring."

He shrugged. "Why should I write them down. God knows what I need. Right?"

"Indeed, He does."

"Then let Him tell you, since He and I don't seem to agree on the things I need." Rocky winced, at the callousness in his voice. He had no right to take his frustrations out on the sweet old ladies, but when they didn't appear to take offense, he let out a soft sigh.

Reba said, "That's a wonderful suggestion, Sonny boy. We'll ask Him to be gracious unto you and provide for your every need, according to His riches in Glory."

He grunted. *Whatever that means.*

Annie clasped her hands under her chin and giggled. "Yes, sister, I do like that. Won't it be fun, to sit back and watch God work His mysterious ways, His wonders to perform?"

Rocky plastered a fake smile on his face, waiting for them to leave, but as the door shut behind them, he was grateful to have found friends who knew nothing about him, yet cared deeply for him. But the true blessing was that they wouldn't be back in the morning, opening his blinds at sun-up and sweeping under his feet.

****

Rocky missed his daughter. He placed a person-to-person, long-distance call to his daughter every Saturday night. Most of the time her grandmother answered and refused it, but even when Cherie answered, she gave a curt "No," when the operator asked if she'd accept the call. What could Dovie have told her to make her hate him? After months of the same response, it seemed as if he could've learned to accept it, but his throat tightened and his eyes filled with tears every time the operator said, "Sorry, sir, the party refuses to accept the call."

He thought of driving down there and trying to talk to her, but he knew Dovie wouldn't allow that to happen and he'd wind up in jail for a trumped up offense. Who would believe him over the old woman whom everyone seemed to think was a saint? How she could've fooled the whole town was beyond his imagination. He could only imagine the lies Dovie had told, but what others in Nearby thought of him was of little consequence. It was what his daughter thought that broke his heart.

The new transistor radio he left on the porch for her sixteenth birthday wasn't returned, yet she never acknowledged receiving it. Rocky felt confident her grandmother found it first, then pretended it was a gift from her. Cherie had always been very gracious. She took after her mother. Even though she was angry, if she had known he left it, she would've at least sent a short note of thanks. Then shrugging, he realized her grandmother probably intercepted all his letters, and if so, Cherie would have no way of knowing his address.

He had shared his frustrations with Becky, who was most understanding for someone who had never had children. It helped to have someone to confide in. Her words were exactly what he would've expected Lilah to say, "Don't give up on her, Rocky. She needs you, even if she doesn't realize it, yet. Go see her."

"Thanks. I will."

She smiled. His mind couldn't wrap around why an upbeat, super intelligent, ultra sweet, compassionate, breath-takingly beautiful woman was unmarried and stuck on the backside of nowhere. It didn't add up. Not that he was complaining. Still, he couldn't help wonder. Most of the males in Kennesaw were either married, elderly or under twenty. Why had she chosen to stay in an out-of-the-way place, instead of moving to Atlanta where she could've someone to share her life with? She had asked for him to tell his story. Why not ask her?

She smiled. "Why are you looking at me that way?" She picked up a napkin and blotted her lips. "Is there something on my mouth?"

"Your mouth is fine. Who are you, Becky Goforth and what is your story?" There. He'd said it.

"My story?" She laughed, which set him at ease.

"I'm not sure I can tell it. Folks here have known me all my life, so no one has ever asked. I don't know how long it might take, but I'll try to give a condensed version."

"Then, you aren't offended that I asked?"

"Offended? I'm flattered that you're interested." Pursing her lips, then blowing out a puff of air, she leaned in slightly and rubbed her hand across her forehead. "Let's see, where should I begin?"

"Start anywhere. You can always go back to the beginning if you leave something out."

"Well, perhaps I should start back around 1882."

Rocky laughed. "I'll have to say, you've aged well."

She smiled. "You laugh, but for you to understand, I think it's a good place to start. I'm trying to put the dates in place and 1882 would be the year Mama Maude was born. Then when she was twenty, her husband was killed and she was left with a three-month-old daughter, she named Lottie. Lottie was my mother. Mother was nineteen when I was born, and that was in 1918. Mama Maude never remarried."

Rocky waited patiently wondering where this was all leading.

"There was no doctor in the little town, and my grandmother was the only midwife. Then in 1939, Mama Maude delivered a baby girl who was rejected by the mother because of a birth defect."

Rocky let out a gasp. He said nothing, yet his mind reeled. How could anyone reject their own child, especially one with special needs?

"My grandmother was instructed to turn the child over to the Welfare Department to be institutionalized, with the explanation that the father was not in the picture and the mother was unable to care for a handicapped child."

"So, the baby became a ward of the State?"

She shook her head. "That would've been the lawful thing."

"I don't understand."

"Mama Maude made out the birth certificate but listed herself as the mother and then wrote in Grandaddy's name as being the baby's father. She named the baby girl Angelina."

"That's a lovely name, but I'm afraid you've lost me. If your grandmother was born in the 1800's wouldn't the authorities have known that she was too old to be conceiving a child in 1939?"

She chuckled. "Well, she was no Spring chicken, but the birth certificate was never questioned." Becky explained her grandmother took the baby and moved to Kennesaw, where no one knew her. The little girl turned out not to be mentally impaired, as first believed, but was only blind.

Rocky's lip turned up at the corner. "Did you say, *only*?"

"Yes! In fact, she appeared to have an unusually high IQ. Then, when the child was six, Mama Maude placed her in a school for the blind in Macon. Unfortunately, my grandmother was diagnosed with cancer and died less than four months after sending the child away to school."

Rocky tried wrapping his head around such a cockeyed story. He glared into Becky's eyes. "You aren't saying—"

"Yes, Rocky, Angel is that baby, but since I'm only 12 years older, it's been less confusing to say we're sisters, rather than to explain a complicated situation. Before Mama Maude died, I made her a promise that I'd raise Angel and see that she graduate from the school in Macon."

Not that it was any of his business, but Rocky couldn't imagine why a grandmother would choose to saddle her young granddaughter with such a heavy burden, and he was quick to say so. Raising a blind child would be a challenge for any parent, and if Angel was six, it meant Becky was only eighteen when she undertook the grave responsibility. Perhaps he should've kept his opinion to himself, but he couldn't help question why Becky's mother wasn't the one designated to raise Angel, instead of placing the burden on the granddaughter who had her whole life ahead of her.

"Burden?" Becky's brow scrunched together in a frown at the mere mention of the word. "Angel has never been a burden. She's always been the bright spot in my life. But to answer your question, my mother died when I was fifteen, so I was the only family member left." She quickly added, "But I would've taken responsibility, even if Mama Maude hadn't designated me. I love Angel, as much as if I had given birth to her. You'll understand when you meet her. She graduates the end of May, and I'm so excited that she'll be coming home soon."

"You say she's sixteen, yet she's graduating? That seems awfully young."

"The blind school doesn't run on the same schedule as public schools."

Rocky felt sorry for Becky before knowing her story, but now he pitied her even more.. She had given up her own life to carry out the wishes of her grandmother. For years, she had worked long and hard at Sam & Sadie's, to pay tuition and board for the handicapped child, who was not even a blood relation. He knew Becky was a special person, but he had no idea how special until now.

Her eyes opened wide. "Hey, what has you so down in the

mouth?"

"I'm just thinking of all you've given up."

"Hey, don't feel sorry for me. When you meet my Angel, you'll realized how blessed I've been. I can't wait for her to meet your daughter, but for that to happen, you need to get on the road and go make things right between you."

"You're right. I hope I can bring her back, but is it selfish of me to ask her to leave her friends in Nearby to come here? Has your sister adjusted?"

Becky smiled. "Adjusted? This is home to Angel. She comes to Kennesaw every summer and on holidays. The folks here know and love her, and she loves them. Sam and Sadie were like grandparents to her. She misses them very much, but she was thrilled when I called and told her you had purchased the café. It would've been difficult for both of us if we'd been forced to move. But our prayers were answered."

Rocky marveled at such compassion, but he couldn't help feeling a bit slighted. Why was God willing to answer everyone's prayers but his? He stopped praying after Cherub slammed the door in his face. Why beg? He was done.

He hurried back to the apartment and packed a duffel bag.

CHAPTER 14

The Court House clock in downtown Nearby struck twelve times as Rocky drove through the little Alabama town on the Florida line. Though he was eager to see Cherie, there was no way Dovie would allow him to see his daughter at such a late hour. He supposed it was best. The trip was tiring, and he'd waited this long. Surely, he could wait a few hours more. He checked into the Osceola Hotel and was given the same room he occupied before driving to Georgia.

He'd expected to fall asleep quickly, yet as many times as he'd gone over the scenario on the trip back, his mind continued to reel. At times, he imagined Cherie would be grateful for the two of them to get a fresh start in a new town. She'd always been a daddy's girl. It would be difficult for her to move away and leave her grandmother. He understood. But the thought of Dovie Albertson raising his daughter sent chills up his spine.

He had to get Cherie out of the old woman's control and

convince her that he loved and needed her.

When the sun finally peeped over the horizon, Rocky crawled out of bed, feeling as weary as he did when he first laid down. Every muscle in his back felt as if someone plaited them together. He dressed and decided to go to the drugstore for a cup of the thick mud Gus called coffee.

Gus reached out and apologized for not being more sympathetic the last time he was there. "I didn't realize it would upset you, since I heard you were the one who walked out on your family. So, naturally I thought—" He rolled his eyes. "Well, I guess I didn't think, or I wouldn't have acted like such an idiot. Forgive me?"

Rocky felt the muscles in his jaw tighten. "I came back, didn't I?" He sat down at the table with the mayor and R.J. Daniels. Gus said, "I reckon you fellows heard. Rocky sold his cottage and plans to move in with Ms. Dovie."

Rocky's jaw dropped. "Me? Live with that woman? Where do you come up with this stuff?"

Gus scratched his head. "But when I said I heard you walked out on your wife, you said, 'But I came back.'"

Rolling his eyes, Rocky said, "But I meant—"

The mayor laughed. "Forget it, Rocky. Gus will change the story ten times before breakfast in the morning. No one takes him seriously."

What difference did it make what people thought? What he

needed was a fresh new start and he'd found the perfect place to make it happen. First, he needed to convince Cherub to agree.

After breakfast, Rocky drove over to the farmhouse and knocked. Cherub opened the door. Her eyes were swollen.

"Hey, angel. I came to wish you a Happy Birthday. I can hardly believe you'll be sweet sixteen in a couple of days. I brought you a present."

"Keep it."

"I can see you're angry. I don't know what your grandmother has told you, but I'm here to set the record straight. Get in the car, sweetheart, and we'll ride over to Graceville and celebrate your birthday early with a plate of fried shrimp."

"I don't need you, so leave me alone." She quickly slammed the door in his face.

Rocky knocked once more, but Dovie opened it. Standing there with her arms planted firmly on her hips and her legs spread apart, she looked like a prison matron prepared to shoot a runaway convict. Then flinging her right arm forward, with her forefinger pointed so close to his mouth he could've chomped down on it, she screamed, "Rocky Stone, get off my property and don't ever come here again."

He rammed his foot in the door when she attempted to shut it. "Dovie, I need to talk to my daughter."

"Are you deaf? She said she wants nothing to do with you, and she's old enough to make up her own mind."

"I have a feeling she had help in making up her mind. Dovie, surely you know you aren't helping her heal by cutting her off from me. That's even cruel for you. Cherie needs me and I need her. You have no right to deny me access to my daughter."

"If you aren't gone in thirty seconds, I'll show you how cruel I can be. I'll have the sheriff here with a restraining order and a warrant for your arrest."

"Arrest? On what charge?"

"Trespassing, harassment, making threatening statements . . . and by the time he gets here, I'll have thought up a few more."

Dovie was mean enough to carry out her threats, and sly enough to fool the whole town into thinking she was some sort of saint. She sat on the second pew from the left every Sunday morning, would yell out an "Amen," a few times, and sway to the music with her hands high in the air. But the woman was as fake as a three-dollar bill. Rocky convinced himself he wasn't judging the old goat, but didn't the Bible say, "By their fruits ye shall know them?" Dovie Albertson's fruits rotted on the vine years ago. The old woman played up to everyone and had them all fooled. Everyone except the man her daughter chose to marry—the man who knew her best.

He had no choice but to walk away and hope that given time, Cherie would figure out that the garbage her grandmother fed her was not because it was true, but because the old woman was a vicious old bird. He laid the wrapped gift at the door and drove away. Cherie was too smart not to figure out her grandmother was the problem. He had to be patient.

****

Dovie Albertson waited for Cherub to leave for school before heading over to the hospital. She hurried down the hall and asked to speak with the doctor.

The nurse said, "I'm sorry, Mrs. Albertson, but the doctor is terribly busy. If you'll have a seat in the waiting room with the other patients, I'll write your name on the list."

Dovie smiled, then with her head cocked, she whispered, Darlin', I'm not here as a patient. I'm sort of a second mother to Coot. She popped her hand over her lips and giggled. "Oh, m'goodness. I suppose I should have said, Dr. Culpepper, but he's been nothing but my precious Coot since he was a wee little thing. I wouldn't ask, except it's very important and something he'll want to know. It'll only take a minute, shug. Now, be a good girl and let him know Big Mama is here and needs a minute or two of his time. He'll thank you for it."

"Yes ma'am."

Minutes later, she saw the doctor walking down the stairs. "Mrs. Albertson, what's going on? The nurse said it was urgent."

She whispered, "It *is* urgent, and I wish you'd call me Big Mama. After all, if things had turned out the way we both wished, I wouldn't have to ask."

He glanced in both directions. "I'm not comfortable evoking such familiarity in a professional setting, especially under the circumstances." He placed his arm around her and walked her into his office. "Now, what's on your mind?"

"It's Rocky."

He turned pale. "You told him?"

"Of course not. And he had no reason to ask."

"I thought he'd left town. I checked at the hotel, and that's the news I got from Abner."

"He did leave, but he came back, wanting to talk to Cherie. "

"Do you know what they talked about?"

"Nothing. She's smart for her age. That girl understands that Rocky is the reason Lilah wanted to end her life. She told him she didn't want to see him and slammed the door in his face. I Suwannee, I've never been so proud of that girl in my life."

"So, your granddaughter knows?"

"Of course not."

"That's good, and I appreciate you wanting to keep me updated, but as I'm sure you saw when you walked in, the waiting room is full. I really need to get back to seeing patients."

"Of course, you do, hon, and I don't mean to keep you. But I thought you might like to know that he was back in town."

"But he didn't ask questions, did he?"

"No. Why would he? As far as he knows, Lilah is dead and buried. This changes nothing."

"What are you talking about? Are you crazy?" Coot paced back and forth. "You conniving ol' woman. You got me into this." He slammed his fist against the desk. "I'm ruined."

"You're blaming me? I don't recall having to talk you into it. You jumped at the suggestion."

He ran his hands through his hair. "You're right. I'm sorry, but you did come up with the cockeyed idea. What was I thinking?" He fell back in his desk chair and buried his face in his hands. "There was no way this could've had a satisfactory ending. I'll lose my license."

"Don't be so dramatic, doctor. It's a bump in the road, but it can still work if you don't panic. We'll go through with it as planned."

"Are you crazy, ol' woman? A bump in the road? I'll never be able to practice medicine again. Please don't come back to the hospital asking for me. If you need to speak to me, you know where I live." He opened the door and ushered her out.

****

Cherub came home from her last day of school and kicked off her shoes, relieved that her grandmother was not home. She supposed it was old age, but Big Mama had become a real grouch, lately. It seemed Cherie could do nothing right. She pulled off her good clothes and put on a pair of dungarees and a tee shirt. The weather was beautiful outside, and she had looked forward to the pool at Lake Nearby opening for the summer.

When her mother was alive, they always marked the calendar for the opening day. But Big Mama had already made it clear she didn't approve of boys and girls bathing together. Cherie tried to tell her they swam, not bathed, but when Big Mama made up her mind about something, she never backed down, even when proven wrong. Cherie said, "But Big Mama, Mama always allowed me to swim in the pool with my friends. *All* my friends."

"Well, your mama is gone, and you now answer to me. I won't have you parading around in a bathing suit in the presence of a bunch of teenage boys, and that's that."

Cherie mumbled under her breath. "I wear swimsuits. Not bathing suits." She trudged to her bedroom and pulled a book from under the mattress. Big Mama didn't approve of her reading novels, which made her want to read the hidden book now, more than ever. She lay back on the bed and opened Peyton Place to the page where she left off. Cherub borrowed the book from Audrey, who got it from Helen. Cherie promised to give it to Judy when she finished. But since she had to sneak around to read it, Judy was becoming impatient.

Cherie went to the pantry and pulled out a brown paper sack. Big Mama saved grocery bags as if paper was going out of style. Cherub and her friends had made covers for their textbooks out of brown paper, decorated with crayons. Her grandmother had remarked it was a clever idea.

She pulled a pair of scissors from the sewing basket, and with a little tape, she had the juicy novel looking like a textbook. No more having to slip around to read. She could go out on the porch, sit in the swing, and finish the book in peace. Just as she was about to sit down, the mailman walked up on the porch.

"Hey, Cherub. I'm running a little late today. I suppose you're glad school is out for the summer?"

"Yessir."

He put three envelopes in the mailbox hanging beside the door and handed an envelope to her. "I believe this one is yours."

"Mine?"

"Yep! You have friends in Georgia?"

"No sir." Puzzled, she reached for the envelope and saw the return address: *Old Stilesboro Road, Kennesaw, Georgia.* She thanked him, then sat in the swing, opened a letter and immediately recognized her daddy's handwriting.

My dearest Cherie,

I know you wonder why I continue to send these letters when you have shown no interest in wanting to hear from me. I suppose this letter will go in the trash, along with all the others, but I had to make one last effort.

Sweetheart, I understand why you feel the way you do, and I understand, but I only wish you knew the truth. Your grandmother has hated me from the first date I had with your sweet mother. I was a nobody, and Dovie felt I was not good enough for her daughter. She was right. I never disputed the fact. I suppose it's the only thing we've agreed upon, other than our love for you and your mother.

Dovie despises me, and her goal has been to turn you against me. She has succeeded and for that, I can never forgive her. I miss you, my sweet girl, and I hope one day you'll forgive me for whatever it is that you're holding against me. But until that day, this will be my last letter. I will attempt to stay out of your life, although it will be the most difficult task I have ever undertaken.

So much has happened since I saw you last. And if you threw the other letters away without reading them, I'll tell you once again, in case you happen to read this. I have moved to a quaint little town in Georgia that feels as if it's straight out of a fairytale book. The people are all so kind and loving. You'll be surprised to learn that I'm now the proud new owner of a thriving café known as The Sam & Sadie. It has a furnished two-bedroom garage apartment in the back, and I had dreams of you sharing it with me the day I bought it. Well, sweetheart, this is it. I won't pester you again. I think of you every time I hear Floyd Tillman on the radio singing, "I love you so much it hurts me," because that's exactly how I feel. The ache in my heart will never go away as long as we're apart.

Goodbye, my angel,

Daddy

CHAPTER 15

Rocky stopped wrapping silverware in the kitchen and ran into the dining room when he heard the commotion. Every customer had left their seat and had their noses glued to the plate glass window. Lloyd yelled, "Her she comes!"

Rocky walked to the door and saw a Trailways Bus stopped in front of the cafe and a beautiful young woman stepped off. At first, he assumed it was Becky's sister, but she wasn't expected for another three days. He realized he was wrong when the girl's face lit up in a smile, she threw up her hand in a wave and hurried toward the café.

Max ran to the kitchen door and yelled, "Becky, she's here."

Becky flung the door open and was outside hugging the young woman before Rocky had a chance to say, "She who?"

Everyone in the café applauded as Becky escorted a beautiful young girl into the cafe. With their arms intertwined, Becky marched her over to the counter. "Rocky, I'd like to introduce you to a real live Angel."

"Angel? You don't mean this is your sister?"

The young woman giggled. "Angelina in the flesh. What's wrong? Am I not what you expected? I'm surprised, because I'd know you anywhere, Rocky Stone."

Becky laughed.

Rocky said, "But I thought . . . I'm sorry, I don't know what I thought."

"Are you wanting to say you thought I was blind?"

He shook his head. "I am. That is . . . I did. But then I saw you wave at Miss Annie." He ran his hand across the back of his neck. "I'm sorry, I don't think I'm making much sense." His brow creased. "Becky, are you sure this is your sister, because I'm pretty sure this beautiful lady can see."

Angel's laugher sounded like tiny bells jingling. "Becky, you were right when you said he's a real looker." Then quickly added, "Oh my. I've made my sister blush."

The room filled with laughter.

Becky said, "I'm sorry, Rocky. I failed to tell you her big mouth often overcompensates for her inability to see with her eyes."

Angel turned and walked straight to Miss Annie and Miss Reba's table, with her hands opened wide. "Hi Memaw and Granny Annie. I was hoping you'd be here."

Rocky whispered to Becky. "How did she know they were there?"

"I'm sure she heard them laugh, and since she knows where everyone sits, she had no trouble finding them."

"She's amazing."

"Didn't I tell you?"

"Yes, but the way she maneuvers between tables without touching one is unbelievable. She's more agile than Coley. He has two good eyes, yet he can't walk across the room without bumping two or three tables on the way."

Coley yelled out, "I ain't deaf. I heard that."

Angel walked over to his table and said, "Get up, you big clumsy lug and give me a hug."

"I was wondering how long it would take you to get to me. We've missed you, baby."

"I've missed all of you, Coley. But I'm home now."

"For good, I hope."

She lifted a shoulder. "Dunno. I'll need a job. I'm qualified to teach, but I've sent out applications in the county and so far, I haven't heard back."

Ralph said, "Don't get discouraged, sweetheart. It may take a while for someone to retire around here but be patient. Something will open up."

Miss Reba said, "Ralph is right, honey. Don't get in a hurry. The Lord will provide."

Rocky rolled his eyes. *Why do they keep saying that?*

Angel said, "I'm sure you're right, Memaw. But I hope it's

soon. I don't want to be a burden on Becky. She's spent the best part of her life taking care of me. It's time I start taking care of myself. I know I can. I just have to convince others."

Rocky had a spur-of-the-moment thought. He hesitated to speak for fear of regretting it later. After mulling it in his head, he shrugged. *Why not?*

He said, "I don't know if this would interest you, Angel, but I understand that before Miz Sadie died, Sam & Sadie's was open for dinner." Heads around the room nodded, along with confirmations of "It sure was . . . yep . . . that's right."

Every eye was on him. It was too late to stop. Sucking in a heavy breath, he said, "I've been thinking. We do a great breakfast business. But if we continued to open from six to eleven for breakfast, with Becky as manager, would you be interested in being night manager and reopening at four in the afternoon for maybe three or four hours?"

Angel bit her lip. "That's very kind of you, Rocky. But I'm not looking for favors."

"Are you saying you don't feel capable of handling the job?"

She chewed on her bottom lip. "Capable? I could do it with my eyes closed."

The room roared with laughter. Ralph yelled, "You tell him, sugar."

Angel said, "I appreciate the offer, but if you don't mind, I'd like to discuss it privately with my sister, first."

"Certainly. I think that's wise. I should've discussed it with her before making the suggestion. There may not be enough interest in the community to serve two meals a day, but Becky would know that better than I would."

Angel laughed. "Two minutes ago, was the first time the thought ever entered your mind. Am I right?"

He shrugged, then realized she couldn't see him. It was easy to forget the girl was blind.

Becky said, "Frankly, I was sorry when Sam decided to stop serving dinner. He insisted it was too much for me to handle. It's not that I have any doubts about Angel's capabilities, but there are other things to consider. She's qualified to teach, and I'm sure an opportunity will open up in the months ahead. Give us a day for her to get settled in, and for us to discuss the pros and cons."

"Sure. There's no rush. Take as much time as you wish. It was just a thought."

****

Relieved when the last patient walked out the door, Coot grabbed his coat and asked Delores, the nurse, to lock up. As he drove up Culpepper Hill, he thought how nice it would be if he could look forward every day to going home to a wife and family. Funny, how for years, a family never crossed his mind. He'd been too busy. Now, the thought pleased him. He wondered if it was Rocky's idea to have only one child—or would Lilah want another baby? After arriving home, he hurried into Lilah's room, greeted her, then leaned over and kissed her forehead. "How's my beautiful girl?"

"Bored! I don't even have memories to think back on. Oh, Coot, how long before I can remember?"

"I know it's difficult but try to be patient." He picked up a novel from off the bedside table. "Perhaps you'd enjoy finishing your book?"

She smiled. "Finishing? I can't even remember starting it. Do I like to read?"

He laughed. "You are a voracious reader."

He placed the book back on the table and took her by the hand. Everything was going better than expected until Coot commented on Lilah's wedding band. Rubbing her hand, he said, "As soon as you're stronger, I'd like to take you to the Jewelers and let you pick out a larger stone."

Her eyes widened. "Coot!"

He smiled. "So, you like the idea, do you?"

"It's not that. For a second, I honestly thought I was on the brink of gaining my memory back. There was a flash of recognition in something you said, but it disappeared before I could grasp it. Oh, Coot, I want so much to remember."

"Don't let it stress you, darling. There's no rush. The past is gone, and a great big, wonderful future lies before us. Isn't that enough?"

Her brows formed a vee. "No. It isn't enough, Coot. I simply have to remember." She ran her hand over her wedding ring. "Besides, I don't need a new ring. I like it. Is it my wedding ring?"

"Probably."

She laughed. "Have you lost your memory, also?"

"I meant, 'yes.' It's a wedding ring, but you need a magnifying glass to find the stone. Wouldn't you like something a little flashier?"

She clinched her eyes shut.

"What's wrong, Lilah?"

"I don't know." Tears fell from her eyes. "I can't explain, but it's as if my memory is sitting there waiting for me to unlock it, and I can't quite reach the key. It happened again when you mentioned buying another ring."

A sick feeling swept over him. *Stone. It was when I mentioned buying a larger stone that she became upset.* There would be no more mention of another ring.

****

As hard as they tried, Coot and Dovie discovered it was impossible to carry out their little charade without bending the truth. One tiny lie had led to another, and another, and each one became bigger, until there seemed to be no turning back.

Dovie had encountered no problem convincing Coot to transfer Lilah from the hospital to his home. In fact, he had jumped at the idea, as if he'd been waiting for her to suggest it. But after two weeks of keeping Lilah shut up in a bedroom, things weren't going as smoothly as they had anticipated. Lilah was asking the wrong questions, but even worse, she was becoming suspicious that she was getting the wrong answers.

Coot and Dovie argued over how to handle the situation. The stress caused a divide between them. Coot was shifting the blame on Dovie, making false accusations and she let him know quickly she wasn't one to sit back and play dead. He was scared and for just reason, but he had no right to turn on her. Although he denied it, Dovie began to believe that Coot had plans all along to move away and take Lilah away from her. He could forget it. It wasn't going to work.

She knew Coot had come back to Nearby with the hopes of winning Lilah back. She even helped promote it. But now, she despised Coot Culpepper almost as much as she hated Rocky.

Dovie drove over to Coot's mansion and rang the doorbell. The maid invited her in. "Come on in, Mrs. Albertson. The doctor's wife has just finished her breakfast and is sitting up in bed. I'm sure she'll be glad to see you. She gets terribly lonely."

"Thank you, Ingrid." There was a time when Dovie would've been thrilled to hear someone refer to her daughter as the doctor's wife, but that was before she knew what a creep the doctor could be. She could see what he was doing, and to think he used her to help him carry out his scheme caused the hairs on her arms to rise.

Dovie grimaced at the thought that it was her idea for Coot to introduce Lilah to Ingrid as his wife who was ill and only recently released from a psychiatric care unit. The woman had come with him from Nashville and was one of the few people in Nearby who wouldn't have known the truth.

CHAPTER 16

Dovey waited for the housekeeper to leave, before she screamed, "You're doing what? Are you crazy? That wasn't the plan. You can't leave town, Coot Culpepper. I won't allow it."

Coot continued to grab Lilah's clothes from the closet and toss them into a suitcase. "I'm sorry, Dovie, but I'm afraid I've allowed you to sway my thinking for the last time. You think this is by choice? Don't you understand? I have no choice."

"You should've considered the consequences before allowing things to go this far."

"But you're the one who had the bright idea." Coot pulled a handkerchief from his pocket and swabbed his sweaty brow. "I'll admit I wasn't thinking straight, but you knew what I was going through, and you took advantage of it. My first mistake was listening to you."

"You're wanting to pin this on me? Try telling that to a jury. I'll have Nearby Alabama's most famous citizen—the renowned

Dr. Sebastian Culpepper—wearing black and white stripes and picking up trash along the railroad tracks on the Samson highway, and don't believe I won't."

"Don't threaten me, ol' woman. You act as if I held a pillow over your daughter's head and murdered her. No one will believe you. As hard as I tried to hide it, I was in love with Lilah, and you know it. Always have been and always will be. Besides, it was your idea."

"Who do you think the people of this town will believe? A loving mother who couldn't bear the thought of never seeing her daughter again? Or the word of a crazed, lonely man who never got over losing the woman he loved to a hog farmer? You can't get by with blaming me, Coot. You know you can't."

"You're crazy, woman. You've had everyone in this town fooled for a long time. Everyone except Rocky Stone. I owe him an apology for not believing the things he tried to tell us about your conniving, manipulative ways."

She cackled. "Yes, please do find Rocky and apologize. When he finds out what you've done, it will probably be the first time he and I have ever been on the same side."

"You're an evil old woman, Dovie Albertson. Pure evil."

"Cross me and you'll see exactly how evil I can be.

"Why are you doing this to me, Dovie, when it was you who came up with the crazy scheme?"

"And who would believe that lie?"

"Lie? *Lie*? You know it was your idea, and you knew how vulnerable I was at the time."

"It will be my word against yours. So, go ahead. Tell whom you may. I have nothing to lose. But what about you?"

She was right. Things had progressed too far to turn around. He should've stayed in Tennessee. He blurted, "I'm ruined. There's no way I can stay in this town, but Lilah is going with me."

"Over my dead body."

"Hey, don't tempt me woman."

"You try to leave with my daughter, and I'll tell her the truth."

"Will you, now? While you're at it, why don't you tell your granddaughter the truth, also? Tell her how you lied to her and let her think her mother was dead."

"Keep Cherie out of this. You can at least allow me to say goodbye to Lilah."

"Fine but be warned. If I go down, you're going with me, so I wouldn't try any funny shenanigans if I were you. You have as much to lose as I do."

****

Rocky walked over to the café thirty minutes before time to open and heard giggling coming from inside the kitchen. He heard Angel say, "Do you think Rocky will go for it?"

"Did I hear my name called? What's going on?"

Angel laughed. "What d'ya mean, boss?"

"Something seems to be terribly funny to you girls. I could

hear the giggling from the top of the stairs. Is the coffee ready?"

Angel said, "Yessir." She pointed to a small table in the corner, set up with a dripolator, a stack of coffee mugs, cream and sugar. "Help yourself, sir."

Rocky's brows meshed together. He glanced over at Becky. "Self-service? You aren't serious."

Becky said, "I can tell by the expression on your face, you don't approve."

"It's not that I don't approve."

"Then what's the problem?"

"I don't mind getting my own coffee, but I don't know how the customers are going to feel about waiting on themselves."

Becky said, "It's Angel's idea. Are you willing to give it a try for three days to see the kind of response we get?"

Angel said, "If we get a single complaint, we'll ditch the idea. All I ask is that you give me a chance to prove the old ways are not always the only ways. I promise . . . one complaint, and we nix the idea."

Rocky scratched his head. "I don't know about this. Do y'all expect them to go to the kitchen and serve their plates, also?"

Angel laughed. "We hadn't considered it, but it might not be a bad idea."

Becky quickly added, "Stop it, Angelina. He'll take you seriously. I'll continue serving Rocky, just as I've always done. I'll also do all the coffee refills, but of course if they choose, they're welcome to go back and help themselves."

Angel said, "Have a seat boss."

"Thanks, but I've got to get my coffee."

"Not yet."

He glanced at Becky and grinned. "She's a bossy little cuss, isn't she?"

Becky laughed, "I like to think of it as strong-willed. It sounds less threatening." She looked up at the clock above the kitchen door. "We still have fifteen minutes before opening the doors. Why not sit down and humor her?"

"Fine, but I hope whatever she has up her sleeve won't take long. I don't have to remind you that I'm a grizzly bear before my first cup of coff—"

Before he had time to finish his sentence. Angel sat a cup of coffee in front of him. He turned and looked at Becky.

Becky said, "Yes, she poured it, brought it to you, and didn't spill a drop."

"How could you tell when it was full?"

"I took home economics at school. We had to learn how to make coffee in a Percolator and pour it to the brim without spilling a drop. Not to brag, but I could do it blindfolded."

Becky laughed but clamped her lips tight when she saw Rocky hadn't caught the humor.

Angel said, "It's really not so difficult, once you get the feel of the pot and know the size of the mug. My ears make up for what my eyes fail to see."

Rocky said, "You ladies seem to know what you're doing. I'll admit, I'm a bit skeptical, but I see Andy and Alice pulling up out front, so it must be time to open the doors." He ran his hand across the back of his neck. "This will be the real test. If Alice doesn't fuss about having to get her own coffee, I'll feel we're home free."

As soon as the door opened, Becky said, "Good morning, folks. The usual?"

Alice said, "Yes, thank you." Then looking somewhat distraught, she said, "Becky, honey, you know how I hate to complain. You try so hard to please, but my toast was a bit dark for my liking yesterday."

"I'm so sorry. I'll make sure the toaster is on a lighter setting today."

"Well, not too light, mind you. I prefer it to be crisp on the outside, soft on the inside, and about the shade of the bark on a crepe myrtle tree. Yesterday it looked more like pine tree bark."

Becky smiled. "Yes ma'am. I believe the second setting on the toaster is the crepe myrtle setting." She waved her arm toward the corner of the room. "Please, help yourself to a cup of coffee, while I turn in your order."

Rocky felt tension in his shoulders, as he waited for the reaction.

Alice's mouth gaped open.

He blurted, "Allow me to bring it to you."

But Alice was already headed toward the table. "A coffee bar.

What a splendid idea. I don't have to guess who came up with such an excellent concept. I'm sure we can thank Angel for this."

Angel laughed. "I knew you'd love it, Miz Alice, since you've always been one to keep up with the latest trends."

"I try, sugar. I certainly try. Rocky, I know you haven't had time to get to know this sweet girl the way we all know her, but she's smart as a whip. Leave it up to the younger generation to improve on what us old fogies have been doing for years."

Rocky said, "I agree, Alice, and you guessed right. I would never have thought of it, but I have no doubt that it's gonna be a hit."

"Indeed, it will, especially among the menfolk, and they're the big coffee drinkers, anyway. They'll like being able to get their own refills when Becky is busy waiting on customers."

Angel said, "Thank you, Mrs. Renfroe. There are always from eight to twelve of the fellows who eat breakfast at home but come in every morning for coffee and conversation. What do you think about the idea of putting a box on the table for them to drop their dime in? That way, they don't have to wait at the register, if Becky is busy."

"Oh m'goodness, yes. That's a great idea. Let's do it. But sweetheart, I don't think a box is the right container. I have just the thing. It's a lovely piece of Mexican pottery and will look great on the table. They can drop their dimes in and leave."

At eleven o'clock, all customers had left except the old-maid Duvall twins. Rocky stood behind the counter talking with Becky and Angel. Becky said, "Rocky, you allowed us to try our idea, but you have the final say. Just because Alice went along with it, doesn't mean you have to. Does the coffee table stay or does it go."

Feigning a frown, he said, "Coffee table? Isn't a coffee table a piece of furniture that sits in front of a sofa to hold a book, a fancy ashtray, and a coaster?" He pinched his chin as if to be mulling it over. "I wonder if you might be referring to the coffee bar?"

Angel laughed. "Yes! The coffee bar. I loved it when Mrs. Renfroe came up with the name. She really liked it, didn't she?"

Rocky chuckled. "I don't try to second guess Alice Renfroe, but I do know she really likes you, Angel. I suspect she would've given her stamp of approval if you'd told her we were going to serve buttermilk instead of cream with the coffee."

Becky said, "Rocky, have you had time to think about what we talked about yesterday?"

"You mean adding a dinner hour?"

"Yes."

"I have, and I know I said we'd talk about it today. But I'd like for us all to take a little more time to consider the ramifications. The idea came off the top of my head. Taking time to mull it over won't hurt a thing."

Angel said, "You don't trust me, do you?"

Becky said, "Angel, that isn't fair. You are quite capable of doing almost anything a seeing person can do. *Almost*. But you do have limitations and Rocky and I need to be completely convinced that allowing you the awesome responsibility of acting as night manager is one which you can handle."

"But I can. I know I can. I've spent hours and hours here with you during summers and holidays. There's nothing a seeing waitress can do that I can't do."

Rocky said, "How will you know when someone walks in?"

"I'm blind, not deaf."

"But once they're seated, then how—"

"Would you like to test me? Go choose a table. I'll wait here."

He shrugged. "I believe you. I don't understand, but I do believe you. We'll need to hire someone to operate the register for you."

"Why?"

Becky said, "I agree there could be problems we haven't considered, but I don't think running the register will be one of them. I can see where it might be if we had tourists stopping in, but our customers are all homefolk."

"I stopped here, didn't I?"

"True! And I'm not saying we'll never have another outsider to stop in, but you've been here long enough to see that it would be rare."

He said, "So, Becky, you have no reservations? You wouldn't be afraid to leave her here, alone?"

"I wouldn't. Everyone in Kennesaw knows her, and our customers will tell her if they've handed her a five or a ten dollar bill. And since she knows which slot each bill denomination goes in, she'll have no trouble making change. She's had lots of experience through the years with me watching over her shoulder. I wouldn't want her to do it if I wasn't confident that she was capable."

Angel said, "I sense you're uneasy, boss. I suggest we not rush into something until we've had more time to consider everything involved. You take all the time you need to think about it, because if you're uneasy, then I'll be uneasy."

"Thank you, Angel. You are an amazing young woman, and I'm already leaning toward saying 'let's do it."

Becky said, "I agree with Angel. Let's wait until we've all had time to think it over. Besides, a little vacation will be good for her. She's worked hard this past year to graduate at the top of her class."

Rocky smiled. "Wow, congratulations, Angel. That deserves a celebration. After we close this morning, I'll carry you ladies to lunch. I hear there's a good catfish restaurant in Sandy Plains. We'll enjoy a good meal together, and maybe even toss around the pros and cons of adding extra hours with a new night manager."

CHAPTER 17

Dovie spoke to Coot's housekeeper, then walked down the long hall to her daughter's room.

"Hi, baby."

Lilah smiled. "Must you call me that. It seems weird hearing a grown woman calling me baby."

Dovie sat down on the edge of the bed. "I'm not just any grown woman. I'm your mama."

"Yes, I remember you telling me. It's just so hard to put it all together. Coot tells me that in time the memories will fall into place. I hope he's right. It's awful when you can't even remember your own family. I know I've been sharp with you, and I apologize. But I have no recollection of being related. Were we close?"

"Very close. I love you so much, Lilah Jean."

"Thank you . . . Mother."

Dovie smiled. "You've always called me Mama. Not Mother."

"Sorry. I'll try to remember. I long for answers, yet I don't know what questions to ask. It's strange the simple things that I can remember, but the things I should remember—the important things—I can't recall. Please, tell me . . . Mama? Who am I?"

Dovie hesitated. Then taking her daughter's hand, she said, "You are my precious daughter and the mother to my grandchild. You and Cherie are my whole life."

"Tell me about my daughter. Coot changes the subject every time I ask about her. All he says is that her name is Cherub and she's away for the summer. I wanted pictures, but he said he left a lot of personal things in a storage unit in Tennessee. What is she like? Does she favor me, or does she look more like Coot? What color is her hair? Her eyes? Is she tall or short, thin or plump? Does she struggle in school or is she smart? Does she play a musical instrument? Is she athletic?" She stopped and giggled. "I suppose I was wrong when I stated that I didn't know any questions to ask. I'm beginning to think of plenty."

"To begin, I'll tell you that she looks nothing at all like Coot. She takes after our side of the family."

Cherub soaked in every word, trying desperately to retrieve the memories as her mother answered all of her questions and told funny family stories.

Dovie said, "I remember the time when Rocky was working on the house, and he sent Cherie to get him a glass of water. She filled up a glass, then ran toward him as fast as she could go. Water was splashing everywhere. Her daddy said, 'Slow down, you're spilling it,' to which she replied, 'if I slow down it will take longer to get there and there will be more time for it all to spill out." Dovie reared her head back and cackled at the memory. But Lilah wasn't laughing.

She said, "Mother, . . . I mean, Mama! Who is Rocky? The name sounds vaguely familiar. It's like it's stuck deep in the crevices of my brain, but I can't dig it out. I don't remember you mentioning the name before. It's odd, because yesterday Ingrid asked if the ring on my right hand was my birthstone. I looked at it and said, 'No, it's rocky.' It was as if I knew what I was saying, but I didn't. It just came out of my mouth."

Dovie's pulse raced. "I declare, that is odd. What do you think you meant to say?"

"I don't know, but certainly not 'rocky.' I fear I'm losing my mind."

Dovie reached over and patted her arm. "Honey, everything will come together in due time, Let it go. It's not worth taxing your brain over."

"Maybe. But I thought of it just now when you mentioned someone named Rocky."

"Did I?"

"Yes. You said Cherie was taking water to Rocky when her daddy told her to walk slow."

"There was no one there but Cherie and her daddy. Perhaps

you misunderstood."

"But I didn't. I'm positive you said Rocky."

Dovie jumped up and glanced at her watch. "Oh, m'goodness, would you look at the time. Gotta go, shug. I left a roast in the oven."

"Oh, I wish you could stay. I've enjoyed talking to you. It's boring being shut up in this room all day, but Coot doesn't want me out among people until my immune system has a chance to recover."

"Your immune system?"

"Yes, from the virus." She laughed. "You act as if you didn't know."

"Oh! The virus."

"He's afraid I'll have a relapse, and we won't be able to go on the cruise."

"Cruise? When did that come about?"

"Apparently he's been thinking about it for some time but didn't want to tell me until he felt I was well enough to go. I'm surprised he didn't tell you."

"He hasn't said a word to me about leaving with you."

"I'm sure he meant to. He's been very busy trying to get his patients all lined up with other doctors, since we'll be gone for a whole month."

****

Miss Annie and her sister were the only ones left in the

restaurant. Rocky kept looking at his watch. His mouth was watering for catfish, and he'd hoped to close a little early, but once Miss Annie started telling one of her tales, she didn't come up for air. He'd never seen a woman who could talk for a solid hour nonstop. Besides, he'd only been here three months, and he'd already heard that same story at least four times.

Becky was counting the receipts. Without looking up, she said, "Ladies, it's time to go. We have somewhere we need to be, and it's time to lock up."

Rocky swallowed hard. He'd never known Becky to be so abrasive. But the old ladies didn't appear to be the least offended.

Reba said, "Oh m'goodness, I hadn't noticed but everyone has left already. Come on, sister, we need to stop by the store and pick up a few cans of cat food for Honeypot."

When the door closed behind them, Rocky ran his hand across his brow. Grinning, he said, "I was ready for them to leave, but I was afraid the sweet ol' soul's feelings would be hurt when you practically shoved them out. However, neither appeared to have been damaged by your curt demand."

Becky laughed. "They're accustomed to having me shove them out the door, and it's always the same response. They are shocked to find everyone has left but the two of them."

Angel said, "What are we doing standing here? I'm starving. I've been thinking about catfish since I awoke this morning."

Just as they approached Rocky's car, Becky said, "That bus is slowing down. I think it's going to stop here."

Rocky said, "All the more reason to leave in a hurry." He was driving away when Becky yelled, "Stop!"

Rocky put on brakes. "What's wrong?"

"A young girl just got off the bus and is walking up to the café."

Rolling his eyes, he said, "She'll discover we're closed."

"That's not the point. She's a stranger, she has a suitcase with her, and her transportation has just pulled away. We can't leave her standing there without finding out if she needs help."

"Maybe she was kicked off the bus. In that case, do we really want to get involved?"

Angel said, "Becky is right, boss. We have to see if we can help her. I'm not as hungry as I pretended to be."

"Aargh! Why couldn't she have come ten minutes earlier or ten minutes later." He backed up in Lloyd's driveway, turned the car around and pulled up to the door of the café. He parked the car, rolled down his window and yelled, "Miss, the café is closed. Can we help you?"

His heart beat like a jackhammer. It couldn't be. But it was. He stopped the car, jerked the door open and ran toward her with open arms. "Cherub?"

She turned around, burst into tears and ran to him, squealing, "Daddy, Daddy!"

****

Dr. Culpepper's nurse lifted her shoulders. "If I've done something wrong, please, doctor, tell me."

"It's nothing you've done, Delores. You're a very qualified, conscientious nurse and I'll be happy to give you an excellent recommendation."

"Then, why?"

"I won't be needing you because I'm closing the clinic."

"Closing? But only for a month. Right? I'll take the month off without pay."

"You're a great nurse, but I won't be needing your services. I'm closing the doors, permanently."

Her brow furrowed. "I don't understand. I know it took a while to get established, but lately we've had so many patients we're scheduling weeks ahead. We need a doctor here, and the folks trust you." Seeing he was not being swayed, she gave up. "What are your plans?"

He lifted both shoulders. "I have none."

"I'm sorry for prying. If you feel you must leave town, I'm sure you have a very good reason for doing so. Maybe I shouldn't say this, but I will. If leaving has something to do with what I think it does, I wish you'd reconsider. The world needs more doctors like you. It would be a shame for you to throw away your career for the love of a woman incapable of loving you back."

His chin quivered. "I'll go ahead and write that recommendation."

"That won't be necessary. For months, the hospital administrator at the hospital in Dothan has tried to entice me into going back, and it's a good place to work. So, please don't worry about me. I'll be fine. It's you that I'm concerned about. If you need someone to talk to, I'm a good listener."

"You're very kind, but talking about it is the last thing I want to do. If you need help carrying your things to your car, I can help."

"Thanks, I think I can handle it. I only have my raincoat, umbrella, lunch box, and pocketbook."

He ambled over to the coat rack to retrieve her umbrella and coat, as Delores picked up her lunchbox and purse. He pretended not to notice the dampness on her cheeks as he walked her outside.

Before getting in her car, she turned around and gave him a hug. "Remember, things are seldom as bad as they seem. I'm sure that whatever is going on, 'this too, shall pass.'"

"You aren't only an excellent nurse, you're a great encourager. But I've made a terrible mistake, and it's one I'll be forced to live with for the rest of my life. I'm such an idiot."

"You're being much too hard on yourself. One mistake doesn't define who you are. You're a brilliant doctor."

He opened her car door, and she slid under the wheel. Then looking up at him, she said, "I'm sorry things didn't work for you in Nearby. I assume you'll be going back to Vanderbilt?"

"Vanderbilt? After what I've done, I'd be lucky if I landed a job as a janitor there. I'm ruined."

Delores said, "Please get in the car. I can see you need

someone to talk to."

"I wish I could."

"I promise it will go no further than the inside of this automobile."

"I believe you, and I appreciate all your kind words, but I'm not ready to talk. I'm too ashamed of what I've done."

"Doctor, I know what it's like to be in love and not have it reciprocated."

He closed her car door and waved her away.

Coot trudged back across the yard, up the steps and stopped in front of the shingle. The new wood had not even had time to weather. He jerked it down, walked into his office and threw it in the trash. He felt he should crawl in the bin along with it. What a mess he'd made.

****

Dovie awoke Friday morning feeling worse than she did when she went to bed. She hadn't slept in a week. The fear of her daughter getting her memory back and discovering that everything she'd been led to believe was a lie, terrified her. Blaming it all on Coot wouldn't fly and she knew it. When Lilah learned the truth, wouldn't it send her straight into the arms of Rocky, since he'd be the only one she could trust? Wouldn't it be easier to go ahead and admit the horrid truth and deal with it, rather than dread the day coming when Lilah would learn how she'd been deceived?

She trudged out of bed, went into the kitchen and made breakfast. Then walking back to her granddaughter's bedroom, she called her, then ambled back into the kitchen. Maybe she should tell Cherie the truth. After all, the whole purpose of not telling her that her mother was alive was because of the fear that she'd tell Rocky.

But now, Cherie was furious with her father and would understand why it was important that he not know the truth. Dovie sat at the table and waited. Finally, she got up, went to Cherie's room to see what was taking her so long. She opened the door and saw a note lying on the bedside table. *"Bye, Big Mama. I've gone to stay with my Daddy. Love, Cherie."*

Dovie's knees were too weak to stand. She fell back on the bed and cried. Then smelling something burning, she jumped up, rushed to the kitchen and pulled a pan of charred biscuits from the oven. Sitting down at the table, she sipped on a cup of coffee. She supposed Rocky had shown up at the house and convinced Cherub that he needed her with him. Cherie was like her mother—she was forgiving to a fault. Dovie knew she would've gone with Rocky willingly, if he showed the least bit of remorse, and she was sure that he used every trick in the book to play on her sympathy.

Dovie drove by the hospital and saw Coot's car parked out front. Good. He wasn't home. She headed over to his house on Culpepper Hill with plans to confess everything to her daughter. She'd tell her she was living with a man who was not her husband. Strange scenarios played out in her head. What if she told Lilah that Coot kidnapped her? Wasn't it the truth? But how would she explain why she waited so long to tell her? Dovie had visited every day for two weeks and never mentioned to her that she was married to another man. Wouldn't that be one of Lilah's first questions? There was no way to reveal Coot as a kidnapper, without revealing the part she played. It was too risky. Lilah would never forgive her.

Coot's housekeeper was outside watering flowers, when she drove up. Dovie got out of the car and waved. "Don't stop what you're doing, Ingrid. I can find my way in. Is my daughter awake?"

"Yes ma'am, and in very good spirits. She's reading and enjoying a second cup of coffee. The pot is still on the stove. Help yourself."

"I've had plenty, thank you."

Dovie walked back to the bedroom and shuddered, seeing Coot's belt lying on a chair. Was he sharing her room? The thought hadn't occurred to her until now. Why wouldn't he? They had convinced Lilah he was her husband. The cad. Lilah might not know better, but he did, and he'd taken an oath to do no harm to his patients. Lilah wasn't his wife, but she was his patient. Lying to her about being her husband was one thing, but Dovie hadn't considered the possibility that he'd stoop so low as to take advantage of her. But what could she do about it? Nothing. She couldn't do squat. Even so, she had to know exactly what was taking place under that roof.

"Good morning, honey." She walked over and picked up the belt. "I guess Coot left his belt when he dressed in here this morning. Should I hang it up in his closet?"

"You can leave it. I'll tell the maid to take it in his room when she comes in."

Dovie felt the air go out of her lungs. "His room? But I assumed—"

"Oh, it's not how it sounds. We aren't having problems, but Coot is very protective of me. Sometimes I feel he's too protective."

"I'm not sure I understand."

"I didn't either when he brought me home. Although I feel perfectly fine, he explained that he doesn't feel we should be intimate until I'm physically and emotionally stable. He insisted on moving all his things from our room into the guest room until he feels I'm stronger."

"But he must feel you're improving, since he's taking you on a cruise. It couldn't be that he might be considering this a sort of honeymoon excursion, could it?"

"I hadn't thought about it. You may be right."

Dovie stiffened. "Don't rush things, darling. I agree with Coot. You should not enter into any extra-curricular activities—if you know what I mean—until you get your memory back. When that happens, then you'll be much more capable of controlling your emotions. I would think excitement or stress of any kind could be devastating to your psyche."

"Devastating to my *psyche*?" She laughed out loud. "I'm not sure I know what that means. Have you always been so protective of my psyche, Mama?"

"Go ahead and make fun of me, but I worry about you."

"I'm sorry. I wasn't poking fun. It just sounded peculiar, but then I have no recollection of any previous conversations you and I have had concerning such an intimate subject. But it made me wonder. What kind of relationship do I have with my daughter? Are we close? Do we discuss such private matters?"

"Very close. Cherie loves you very much."

"I'm glad. I wonder what's keeping Coot. I thought he'd be here before now. We have to catch a plane to Miami at seven-forty-five this evening. We'll spend the night there, and our ship will leave at eight-thirty in the morning."

Dovie's throat tightened. She wanted to scream, "Don't go," but she could think of a dozen reasons why she couldn't. "Are you sure you feel like going?"

"I'm still quite weak, but Coot says the cruise will do me good. He plans to take off the month of July to celebrate my coming out of the coma. He'll open his practice back up in August."

"As soon as Coot can get her college mailbox number, I want to write Cherie and let her know that her father and I are extremely proud of her for winning the scholarship, and to tell her how badly I feel about being in a coma when she left for summer school. I wish I could've seen her before she had to leave. It's so difficult to believe I have a daughter in college."

Dovie's jaw tightened. She heard Coot clear his throat and looked up to see him standing in the doorway. Feigning a smile, she said, "Yes, it's difficult for me to believe, also. I hardly remember her senior year, myself."

CHAPTER 18

Rocky picked up his daughter's luggage and said, "I have someone I'd like for you to meet." They strolled toward Becky and Angel, and after he made the introductions, he said. "Ladies, please forgive me but I need to give you a raincheck on that lunch. I'd like to spend time with my daughter. Her trip here has caught me by surprise—a great surprise, I might add. I hope you understand."

Becky said, "Absolutely, we understand. And she is just as beautiful as you claimed, Rocky."

Cherie smiled. "Thank you, but what's this about lunch?"

Rocky said, "It was no big deal. We were headed over to a catfish house, but we'll do it later. You and I have a lot to catch up on."

"Not on an empty stomach. Let's all go. I'm famished."

Angel laughed. "I thought you'd never suggest it."

"It was a long trip. I left on the bus last night at 9:30, then we had a long layover in Montgomery. I only had enough money for a pack of cheese crackers and a grape soda, so I'm starving."

Becky sat up front with Rocky, and the two girls sat giggling in the back seat, as if they'd been best friends forever.

The restaurant was crowded, but the wait was less than fifteen minutes. The two teenagers took a walk along the edge of the nearby lake, while waiting to be called. When they sat down to eat, Cherub said, "Angel and I are discovering we have so much in common."

Angel nodded. "I think I've found my soul-sister."

Cherie said, "I feel the same way, but you know what's weird?" Not giving anyone a chance to answer, she said, "Angel is blind."

Angel feigned shock. Pounding her hand over her heart, she groaned. "Oh no. Tell me it ain't so. Blind?"

"Silly, I meant I didn't have a clue until you told me. Now, that's really weird. I mean how did we carry on a lengthy conversation on the way here, and then walk down the lake, and me not realize that you couldn't see?"

Angel said, "Maybe you're the one who is blind?"

"Funny!" Then looking a bit skeptical, she said, "Wait. You aren't really blind. Are you? You were pulling my leg, weren't you?"

"Pulling your leg? Could've been. Or was it your arm? I'm blind. Remember?"

Rocky didn't understand what prompted Cherub to make the

long trip on a bus, but hearing the giggling made him feel everything was gonna be fine.

After arriving back at the café, Becky and Angel were getting ready to go home, when Angel yelled for Cherie to wait.

Cherie stopped. "What's wrong?"

"Nothing. I think I already know what you look like. I have a vision in my head, but I want to 'see you' with my hands. Do you mind?"

Cherie reached for Angel's hand and placed it against her cheek, then waited as the soft fingers caressed every inch of her face.

Angel said, "My fears have just been confirmed."

"Fears? What fears?"

"I was afraid you were prettier than me, and now I know it's true."

Cherie laughed and threw her arms around her, giving her a hug. "It's not true. You are much prettier."

Becky yelled, "Angel, I need to go. You and Cherie will have all summer to be together."

When Rocky walked Cherie up the stairs to the apartment, she oohed and ahhed, declaring it to be the cutest apartment she'd ever seen. "Oh, Daddy, I love my room. We studied different styles of furniture in home economics, and French Provencial was my favorite. Isn't it purely divine?"

Rocky laughed at her choice of words. He was glad she approved, but he was especially thrilled to hear her refer to it as 'her room.' His hopes had just been confirmed. She had come to stay, but the anticipation of what brought about this change in attitude was peculiar. He could hardly wait to hear her story. "Is your grandmother ill?"

"Ill? Boy, is she ever. When has she not been ill? I can never do anything right in her eyes."

"I meant ill as in sick and needing medical care."

"Oh. No sir. She feels fine. But she's been on a real high horse lately, and frankly, I took it as long as I could. I hope you aren't angry, Daddy."

"No, sugar. I'm not angry. I've missed you more than you could ever know. I'm excited that you're here with me. I was just wondering what Dovie had to say about you coming here."

"I didn't ask her, but I have a good idea what she would've said if I had told her I was coming."

"Are you saying she doesn't know you're here?"

"She knows by now. I left her a note. You are angry, aren't you?"

"No. You have every right to be here. I'm trying to sort things out in my mind. That's all. You never answered any of my letters, although I kept sending them. And the last time I saw you, you literally slammed the door in my face and demanded that I leave you alone. I'm wondering what happened to cause this shift in your feelings toward me."

"I'm sorry, Daddy. I wouldn't blame you if you hated me. I was mixed up."

"Honey, I promise I'm not upset with you, but I need to know what changed."

"I did. I finally realized Big Mama had been lying to me about a lot of things."

"Such as?"

"She claimed you didn't love me and that the only reason you hung around as long as you did, was because you were hoping she'd die and with Mama gone, you'd inherit the farm. She told me she's willed the farm to me, and that I'm not to let you step foot on the grounds. She hates you, Daddy, and she poisoned me against you. That is, until I found out the truth."

"And how did that happen?"

"The only letter from you that I ever saw came yesterday. After reading it, I realized that she lied to me when she said you didn't love me. Big Mama always goes to bed before nine o'clock, and since the bus was leaving at 9:30, I slipped out the front door with my bag and walked to the bus station. And here I am."

"You know she'll be looking for you, to take you back. You'll need to be strong. Do what you feel in your heart is right. If that means staying here, I'll be thrilled. But if you feel you need to be with your grandmother, I promise to understand. I won't hold it against you."

"Being with Big Mama is the last thing I need, Daddy. Please don't send me back."

"Baby, I would never, ever send you back. If you leave, it will be your decision. I need you."

"Do you, Daddy? I want to believe you, because I haven't felt needed by anyone in a very long time."

"Sweetheart, it's no secret your grandmother and I don't see eye-to-eye on things, but there's one thing we have in common: We both love, want, and need you in our lives."

"That's not completely true, Daddy. I'm nothing but a pawn to Big Mama. She uses me to get back at you. I don't know why it took me so long to see it, but I don't think she even loved Mama as much as she pretended."

"No. No, no, no. I don't care for the woman, and I can't believe I'm standing here defending her, but if there's one thing I'm sure of, it's that she worshipped Lilah. She gave up living in a big, fine house to live in cramped quarters, for no other reason than to be with you and your mother. Honey, it's me that she doesn't like."

"You don't know her as well as you think, Daddy. I believe some people are driven by hate, and Big Mama is happiest when she has someone to hate. Now, she'll be twice as happy, since she can hate us both."

Rocky walked over and placed a palm on either side of his daughter's face. "Listen to me, sweet girl. It would be impossible for anyone to hate you. Perhaps I've spoken against Dovie in front of you at times when it would've been wise to have kept my mouth shut. So, if I'm the cause of you feeling the way you do toward her, I apologize. The problems between your grandmother and me have nothing to do with you. Nothing whatsoever. Do you understand?"

"I understand, Daddy, but I'm afraid you're the one who doesn't get it. Big Mama is sick. Sick in the head."

"Honey, you're angry, and anger can weigh you down. Let it go. Even if it were true, I wouldn't want you carrying such bitterness in your heart. It's a heavy load." He let out a soft whistle. "I should know."

****

Dovie Albertson stuck Cherub's note in her pocketbook and trekked down to the police station. "I'd like to report a kidnapping. My sixteen-year-old granddaughter was snatched while I was gone, and I am absolutely frantic."

Chief Wooley's brows formed a vee. "I can certainly understand why you would be."

"Tom Wooley, you've sworn to uphold the law by prosecuting criminals, am I right?"

"Yes ma'am. I took the oath to protect the citizens of Nearby, and I take my job seriously."

"That's good to hear, because I'll expect nothing less. I realize Rocky is one of your fishing buddies, but I want him found and prosecuted to the full extent of the law."

"Hold on. Are you suggesting your son-in-law has taken your

granddaughter?"

"It's not a suggestion. It's a fact and I'm here to file a claim against him. He's kidnapped Cherie."

"I see. Please have a seat, Mrs. Albertson, and Officer Allred will take down the information, as soon as he finishes eating."

"Excuse me?"

"I said the officer will be with you shortly."

She pointed to the officer behind a glass partition. Then with her hands planted firmly on her hips, she screamed, "My granddaughter is missing, and you expect me to sit here and wait for Gordy to finish licking the icing off his chocolate Twinkie? What kind of station are you running here?"

Officer Allred licked his fingers, then walked out offering his apologies. "Did I hear you say your granddaughter is missing?"

"That's correct."

"How old is she, ma'am."

"You know how old Cherie is. Stop acting like you have no idea who I'm talking about."

"Just the facts, ma'am. When did you see her last?"

"She went to bed early last night. But since it was her first day of summer vacation, I decided to let her sleep late. I called her to breakfast at nine o'clock, and she had already been abducted."

"Jumping Jehosophat, woman. You're wanting to put out an APB on a teenager who has only been missing for a few hours? Go home and wait for her."

The chief hid his lips. "Officer, Allred, we have reason to believe the young woman in question has been abducted by her father. His name is Rocky Stone."

He stepped back and cocked his head to the side. "Rocky? You aren't serious. Are you, Chief?"

"I think you should follow up."

"Aww, Chief, you don't really think—"

Dovie stomped her foot. "Don't think I didn't see that smirk, Gordy Allred. If it was Ellie, missing, I'm sure you'd want every officer in the county looking for her."

"Sorry, Miz Dovie. I didn't mean to make light of the situation. But I know Rocky, and I know he loves his kid. If you have reason to believe she's gone somewhere with her daddy, I fail to see the urgency. Rocky probably took her over to the Tasty Freeze for a chocolate malt. I wouldn't be surprised if she doesn't beat you home."

"She has no plans to come back. That's why I want you out looking for them. Rocky's last known whereabouts was somewhere in Georgia."

"Georgia? Now that you mention it, I haven't seen him around lately."

"There's no telling where he's headed with my granddaughter."

Gordy rubbed the back of his neck. "Is there anything more that you haven't told me?"

"No. Just find her. I wouldn't put it past him to head out of the country with her." Then, popping her palm against her cheek, she said, "Oh. I didn't mention the note, did I?"

"Note? You aren't saying he's seeking a ransom in exchange for Cherie, are you?"

"Of course not. You've been watching too many Dragnet shows on TV."

"May I see the note?"

He read it. Frowned. Then read it a second time. The frown disappeared and he let out a hearty belly laugh, before tossing the note over to the chief. "What's the charge when a sixteen-year-old goes to visit her father and leaves a message of her whereabouts?"

She jerked her head back, emphasizing her indignation. "I am appalled at your attitude."

"Aww, Dovie, go home. Your granddaughter hasn't run away, and you know it. She's with her daddy. She's in no danger."

"That's what you think. But if I have to go all the way to Montgomery and talk to the Governor to get action, I will. I want my granddaughter back home where she belongs."

Dovie muttered to herself all the way home, saying all the brilliant things she wished she would've said to Tom and Gordy, and rehearsing the things she'd bring up at the next City Council meeting. "When I get through, Gordy and Tom may find it hard to get a job digging potatoes."

She headed straight for the trash can beside the house, before going inside. She had hopes of

finding one of the letters Rocky had sent to Cherie, to see if there was a forwarding address on the envelope. If only she could remember the postmark. She was positive it was somewhere in Georgia, but nothing came to mind. Maybe she was putting too much emphasis on Georgia. As far as she knew, he had no relatives there, so the chances that he would've stayed there were slim.

She vaguely remembered him once saying he had distant kinfolk in Mississippi. Dovie grabbed the phone and called Chief Wooley. "Tom, I think I know where they are?"

"Who?"

"Rocky and Cherie, of course."

"Good. I'm glad you found them."

"I haven't found them. I called to tell you where to look."

"Aww, Dovie, give it up. No crime has been committed."

"Are you saying you aren't even going to pursue the case?"

"That's exactly what I'm saying. Now, I don't mean to be rude, but we're in the middle of a game of Hearts, and it's my turn. Bye."

The chief hung up and cackled as he grabbed his coat off the rack. "I'm outta here, boys."

Gordy said, "What's so funny?"

"That was Dovie on the phone. She called to give us a tip that Rocky might be visiting relatives somewhere in Mississippi."

"What did you tell her?"

"I told her we were busy playing Hearts and didn't have time to talk."

Gordy and Hal eyed one another. "Hearts?"

"Yeah. It was the first thing that came to mind. She needed something to get her mind off Rocky. I figured that would do it. Have a good evening, guys. I'm heading over to the County Lake to wet a hook."

CHAPTER 19

Lilah waited impatiently for Coot to come home. She could hardly wait to walk around and to see the outside world again. She was tired of lying in bed, depending on someone to constantly do things for her that she felt physically able to do for herself. Coot promised that once they were on the ship, they'd sit on the deck and the sunshine and fresh air would be the medicine she needed. He sent her picture and body proportions to an image consultant at Bloomberg's in Dothan to choose a proper trousseau for her to wear on the cruise. Lilah had never seen so many beautiful outfits. Or had she?

Was Coot tired of all her questions? Did he really understand how frustrating it was not to remember anything? The front door opened, and she heard him yell. "Where is my beautiful Lilah?"

She giggled. "Where do you think I am? I'm in the bed, but I am so ready to blow this joint."

Yelling back, he said, "I'm glad to see you're in a good

mood."

"I'm too excited to be any other way. Ingrid has my bags packed and I can't wait to leave."

Ingrid walked in holding a navy blue suit and white blouse. "Is Madam ready to dress?"

Coot said, "Yes, thank you, Ingrid. While you get her ready, I'll go ahead and put our luggage in the car. Call me when you're through, and I'll take her to the car."

Lilah said, "Coot, you promised that when it was time for the trip, you'd treat me as your wife and not as your patient."

"So, I did, sweetheart, and I look forward to keeping that promise. But the trip begins when we board ship."

Ingrid was helping Lilah dress, when she said, "It's been a pleasure tending to your needs, Mrs. Culpepper. You're not only a beautiful lady, but you have a beautiful soul." She whispered, "Don't go."

Lilah giggled, then hugged the woman who had hovered over her from the day Coot brought her back home. She thought about all the times she had wished Ingrid would simply keep house and not be so attentive. Now, she realized how fortunate she was to have such a sweet caretaker.

"You're a jewel, Ingrid."

Again, whispering, she said, "Please?"

"I beg your pardon?"

"Please don't get on the ship. Things are not as they seem."

Her pleading made no sense. "I've never been on a cruise, but I'm looking forward to going. I know you don't think I'm well enough, but honestly, I feel fine. Besides, I'll have a fabulous doctor with me every minute of the day."

"But there are things you don't know."

"You're right, but Coot seems to think in time, everything will begin to make sense."

Coot walked in. He held out his hand toward Ingrid. "You've been terrific. Thank you for all you've done for Lilah."

Lilah said, "I'm hoping when we return from the trip, your duties will be housekeeping only and won't include caretaking."

Ingrid looked at Coot. "When you return? But I understood Dr. Culpepper to say—"

Coot raised a brow. "You're dismissed, Ingrid."

"Yes, doctor." She hung her head and ambled out of the room.

Lilah said, "Honey, Ingrid has been so good to me. I hope you didn't hurt her feelings."

"What did I say?"

"It was how you said it. You didn't let her finish her sentence before interrupting her in a very abrupt manner. It wasn't like you."

"You're too sensitive. Ingrid worked for me when I lived in Nashville. She probably knows me better than anyone, since she's been with me for years."

"Maybe so, but I still think it was rude of you to cut her off when she was talking."

He smiled. "Maybe I was a little curt with her. I apologize."

"You're apologizing to the wrong person."

"Lilah, I'm a grown man. I don't need you or anyone else correcting me or giving me etiquette instructions."

Her throat tightened. He had never talked to her in such a brusque tone. Or had he? She rubbed her temples, as if doing so would help stir her brain into recalling her past life.

Coot put his arm around her waist, as he helped her to the car. "Our plane leaves Pensacola for Miami at seven-forty-five this evening. We don't need to waste any more time."

"I've forgotten what time our ship leaves."

"Eight-thirty tomorrow morning."

Lilah was quiet as Coot drove past the Florida line. She read the Burma Shave signs along the way, but her mind wasn't on the cute little ditties. Ten or twelve miles down the road, Coot said, "You're awfully quiet. What's wrong?"

"Nothing."

"Surely, there's something bothering you. You were all giddy when I came home. It was good to hear such excitement in your voice. But now, you seem to have snuck into a shell. If there's something bothering you, I'd like to know. Maybe I can help."

"I don't think you can. I don't think anyone can help me."

"Try me."

"Mama said when I was little, someone named Rocky gave me

a glass and told me to fill it with water. But when I asked who Rocky was, she acted as if she didn't know anyone by that name."

Coot stared straight ahead. "So, you think your mother was lying? What reason would she have?"

"I didn't say she was lying."

"That's what it sounded like to me."

"She acted as if I made it up, but I distinctly heard her."

"Obviously your mother didn't say what you thought she said, else she would remember. She's not senile."

"And I'm not deaf. I know what she said."

"Have you ever known anyone by the name of Rocky?"

He laughed. "Have you?"

"I don't know. It sounds vaguely familiar." She rubbed her temples. "I can't seem to get it out of my head."

Coot slammed the palm of his hand on the steering wheel. "I've had enough! "Lilah, if you plan on getting all melancholy over something you can't explain, we might as well turn around and go home. I hoped this would be a sort of honeymoon cruise, but it won't be if you're more interested in recalling the past than enjoying the present.

"Did we not have a honeymoon?"

"Not a honeymoon cruise."

"Where did we go?"

"Good grief, there you go again, wanting to live in the past. Forget the past, it's gone. You don't remember it and I choose not to."

"Why? Were we not happy before?"

He pulled over to the side of the road and stopped the car. "Lilah, do you trust me?"

"You know I do."

"Then, please trust me when I tell you it's for your own good that we look forward and not backward. We have a great big, beautiful future ahead of us, but if you insist on trying to live in the past, I'm truly afraid you'll wind up in the hospital again."

"Are you saying I should stop trying to remember my life before the coma?"

"That's exactly what I'm saying. The past is a closed book, and we are about to embark on an exciting new chapter the moment we step on the ship. There'll be no reason for either of us to ever turn back the pages." He looked at her and winked. "Doctor's orders. Is it a deal?"

She slid close to him and nodded. "Deal!"

****

Dovie Albertson went to the Women's Quarterly Meeting at Hazel's house. She never quite understood why they called it a quarterly meeting when they met the third Tuesday of every month, but no one dared change the name. Lena had been President for the past eleven years, but after her passing in February, the women voted for Dovie to be the new President.

After calling the meeting to order, she said, "Ladies, it's our custom to have the program before prayer time, but I have a very special reason for wanting to switch things around. My heart is burdened this morning, and I'm standing in the need of prayer. My daughter is gone, and I haven't slept for a solid week." Her eyes searched the expressions, and her gut told her she was right.

There wasn't a woman in that room who hadn't heard her own set of rumors concerning Lilah's demise. With the exception of sweet, naïve Pearl, anyone who knew Dovie would know it would be out-of-character for her to mourn her daughter's death quietly or refuse a big church funeral.

Lucy walked over and placed her arm around Dovie. "We were all saddened by your loss, hon. Those of us who haven't lost a child can't possibly understand the pain you're going through, but our hearts and prayers are with you."

"I didn't lose her."

"I beg your pardon?"

"I know where she's gone."

Thelma said, "Of course, you do, and we all know, too."

Every head in the room nodded.

Dovie said, "My daughter didn't go to heaven."

Thelma's jaw dropped. "That's the old devil wanting you to believe that, Dovie. Rebuke it. We all knew Lilah, and no one loved the Lord any more than your sweet girl."

"Amens," were murmured throughout the room.

Dovie was keen enough to know the stunned looks on the faces were fake, since bad news in Nearby circulates around town at least thirty minutes before it even happens. She was quite sure everyone in the room had either heard or made up their own set of rumors. Everyone in town over thirty could remember when Coot was sweet on Lilah in high school. With both Coot and Lilah missing at the same time, there was not much way to skirt the truth.

Dovie had managed to fool Cherie and Rocky into believing Lilah was dead, but she couldn't fool the whole town. Rumors were circulating and she knew it. What would happen if Lilah should suddenly regain her memory? How could she have thought it was a good idea to trick her granddaughter into believing her mother was dead? What was she thinking? Swallowing hard, she answered her own question: She wasn't thinking. Would Cherie understand if she said, "My hatred toward your daddy drove me crazy? I must've been out of my mind?"

Hazel raised her hand. "Dovie, are you okay?"

She looked out at the women staring at her and nodded. "I'm sorry. I lost my train of thought. What did you say?"

"You don't look well. I'm in charge of the program, but I think we should spend all of our time today praying for you. Is there anything you'd like to share to help us know how better to pray for you?"

"Thank you, Hazel, but I hardly know where to begin. Suppose you all tell me what you've heard about Lilah, and together maybe we can piece together the truth."

Dovie's suspicions were confirmed by the guilty looks on the faces around the room. "Thelma, suppose you go first." She knew which one to call on, since nothing ever got past Thelma.

Thelma looked around the room. "Well, you know how I hate to spread gossip, Dovie, and I'm sure there's nothing to this, but they say she was in the hospital, but when Doc Coot closed the hospital, it left some folks concocting their own version of what happened. They say Doc Culpepper transferred your daughter to Bryce Hospital."

Jennie threw up her hands, "They say? They say? Who is 'they,' Thelma. That's pure crazy. Dovie's sweet Lilah passed away at the clinic. Why would Doc send a corpse to a mental hospital? Anyone who believes that garbage is the crazy one."

Lucy said, "I heard Lilah had amnesia before she died, but I didn't believe it. Besides, I don't think there is such a thing. I have a feeling that folks who claim to have amnesia are hiding something and it's their way of pretending they don't remember."

Hazel said, "I'm sorry, Lucy, but you are misinformed. Amnesia is a real sickness. It appears we've all heard different stories, so why don't we let Dovie give us the details, so we'll know better how to pray."

Pearl, never one to indulge in gossip, raised her hand. "I heard Lilah was in a coma. I prayed that she'd wake up. We don't always understand God's ways, but we know He never makes a mistake."

A shrill sound caused the ladies to grab at their ears. Cora sat trying to adjust her hearing aid. She blurted, "Pearl, did you say she's dead? Oh, Dovie, hon, I'm so sorry. I heard Lilah was sick, but I hadn't heard about her death. When's the funeral? I vote we send flowers from the group."

Hazel leaned over and yelled in Cora's ear. "Dovie hasn't been well, lately, so there's been no funeral. I'm sure she'll want to have a memorial service later, when she's up to it.

Dovie rapped a gavel on the podium. "Excuse me ladies, but I can see there's a lot of misinformation going around. The truth is, my sweet Lilah is alive—"

She paused, hearing the gasps. "I wish I could say alive and well, but unfortunately she's very sick." She almost added, "But not as sick as I," but they would determine that quickly enough.

Hazel walked over and patted Dovie on the back. "True. Christians never die, but live eternally in a better place. I can see this has all been too much for you to bear. But hon, your baby is well. She's no longer sick. It just doesn't seem right for a mama to have to bury her child, but we'll understand it better by and by."

Lucy said, "Hazel is right, Dovie. I love that song." Lucy sang a few bars of ". . . trials dark on every hand, and we cannot understand. But we'll understand it better by and by." A few ladies joined in and agreed it would be a lovely song to be sung at Lilah's funeral.

Hazel said, "Dovie, Lilah once told me she loved to hear me sing Sweet Beulah Land, and I'll be happy to help you plan a nice service for her when you're ready."

Thelma said, "Ladies, I think if Dovie needs our help, she'll ask for it."

Dovie shook her head slowly. "Please stop all the talk about a funeral. Lilah is alive."

Hazel crossed her arms over her chest. "Well, of course she is, hon. After Jesus was crucified, Mary said to the disciples, 'He's alive and I've seen him.' But did they believe? No."

Lucy said, "Hazel, no one here would dispute that Lilah was a saint, but she wasn't Jesus."

Hazel's brow shot up. "I didn't say she was. What's your point, Lucy?"

Dovie was glad in a way that they continued to bicker. It had given her opportunity to decide what and how much she needed to share. "Ladies. Please hear me out. Thelma, you heard correctly. Lilah suffers from amnesia, and Hazel is correct in saying that it's indeed real. Lilah has no recollection of her past. She would never pretend not to know me or her daughter, but it broke my heart when I had to introduce myself."

Cora said, "How is your granddaughter holding up, since losing her mother? Bless her heart."

Thelma said, "Cora, put your hearing aid back in. Dovie is trying to tell us Lilah is alive."

"Did you say someone lied?"

The murmuring grew loud. Hazel shouted, "No one lied, Cora. Now, please let Dovie talk."

Dovie said. "But someone has lied, and she's standing in front of you. Pearl, God heard your prayers. However, as soon as Lilah woke up, she was transferred to a private home where she has been under the watchful eye of a caretaker. She is presently on a cruise, recommended by her physician." Dovie's heart pounded so fast, she thought at times she could actually hear it thumping. She had managed to tell the truth. Maybe not the whole truth, but more than she started out to tell. Now that she had said it, she felt a heavy burden had been lifted.

Thelma said, "I've never lived in a place that spreads as much gossip as this town. It's scandalous the way folks talk around here."

Lucy said, "You're the one who told me Lilah lost her mind and was secretly shoved off to Bryce Hospital."

Dovie said, "I had no idea there were so many stories circulating. I'm glad we took the time to clear things up."

Hazel said, "Before we pray, tell us about your granddaughter. My Betsy told me Cherub left town. I suppose she went with her mother on the cruise?"

Dovie shook her head. "No. Cherie is spending time with her father."

"Oh, dear. I'm sure that's hard on you. I know you aren't fond of Rocky."

"You're right, but Cherie needs to discover for herself what that man is really like. She's always been under the false impression that Rocky Stone could do no harm. It won't take long for her to learn the truth and to come back home where she belongs."

Hazel jumped up. "My goodness, I had no idea it was so late. The time has slipped away from us. Thelma would you please help me serve refreshments?"

Cora said, "I know I don't always hear well, but did we pray already?"

Thelma shrugged. "Pray when you get home. We need to serve the cake before the icing melts. I made it with Dream Whip and lime Jello. It's a new recipe."

Dovie thought it peculiar that no one questioned Coot's whereabouts, especially since he and Lilah went missing at the same time. Thelma brought her a crystal dessert plate containing a lime green, three layer cake, two cheese straws, a few strawberries, and a cup of Russian Tea.

She realized she had fretted far more than was necessary. She had told the truth, and no one would be shocked when Lilah returned. Now there was nothing left to do but wait. Wait for her daughter to return. Wait for Lilah to regain her memory. And wait to hear from Cherie.

There were several things Dovie felt confidant she could do and do well. She was a great seamstress, she could play a piano, carry a tune, and she was known throughout Nearby for her chicken 'n dumplings. But the one thing she wasn't good at was waiting.

CHAPTER 20

Friday night Cherub invited Angel to spend the night. At two o'clock in the morning, Rocky stumbled into his daughter's room and demanded they keep the laughter down in order for him to get a few hours' sleep.

After he went back to bed, Cherub said, "Let's take the quilt and our pillows outside, so we won't have to be quiet." But it didn't take long for the laughter to subside, and the conversation drifted away from boys as the girls shared their hopes, dreams, and their biggest fears.

Angel said, "Why don't we play a game. I'll ask you something I want to know about you, and then you ask me a question."

"I like it. But we can ask anything, right?"

"Sure. You go first."

"How long have you been blind?"

"From birth. Now, it's my turn. What happened to make you

leave your mother to come here?"

"She took rat poison and died."

Angel laughed. "Seriously, what happened?" The sudden silence caused Angel to cover her mouth with her hand. Her voice quivered. "You're serious? Oh m'goodness, Cherie, please, please forgive me. That must've been awful for you."

"It has been."

"You must hate me for laughing. I had no idea."

"It was my fault. I shouldn't have been so blunt. Sometimes it makes me angry when I think about what she did. But Mama and I were very close. Now, what about your mother. Is she dead?"

"I have no idea. She didn't want me."

Cherie popped her hand over her mouth. "That can't be true."

"But it is."

"Do you remember her?"

"No."

"That is so sad. I'm sorry, Angel."

"Thanks, but don't feel sorry for me. I've had a decent life, but I do wish I could've known her. I suppose that sounds odd, since she didn't want me. I've always wondered if she didn't want me because I was blind, or if she wasn't married. Now, I have a question for you, but you'll laugh."

"Good. I like it when you make me laugh. What's the question?"

"How would you feel if my sister and your daddy were to fall in love?"

Cherie shrieked. "Wouldn't that be so wild? We'd be sisters." Then with a shrug, she said, "But I don't see that happening. Daddy is still crazy in love with my mother, even though she's gone."

"And he'll always love her. But we'll both be leaving home in a couple of years. I know you don't want him to be lonely, and I don't want Becky to live the remainder of her life as a lonely spinster."

"She doesn't act as if she's lonely."

"She puts on a good show. Every time I hear The Platters sing 'The Great Pretender,' I feel as if they wrote it about Becky. It fits her so well." She flung her head back and the words flowed from her lips. "My need is such, I pretend too much. I'm lonely, but no one can tell."

"Oh, Angel, you have a beautiful voice. I wish I could sing like you. I love your sister, but it wouldn't work. It's too soon for Daddy. He's still in mourning. Frankly, I don't think he would've bought the café if he'd been thinking straight."

"What's wrong with the café?"

"Nothing. I love it, and I'm glad we're here. I'm just saying that Daddy normally thinks things through very carefully before making a decision. I really believe it was the grief that caused him to do something so spontaneous. It's out of character for him."

"Do you have regrets?"

"Not at all. I'm thrilled. I think he needs to have something in his life to make him want to get out of bed every morning."

Angel said, "Exactly. And so does Becky. It's my fault she's still single. I don't want her to wind up like Miss Annie and Miss Reba, but that's the direction she's headed."

"You're being too hard on yourself. It's not your fault."

"But it is. Becky was eighteen and engaged to be married when her grandmother—who adopted me at birth—died. Becky petitioned the courts to gain guardianship of me."

"Then you and Becky aren't really sisters?"

"No, but it's easier to say we are than to explain to people."

"So, why would you think it's your fault that she never married?"

"Because when her grandmother was dying, Becky promised her she would raise me. The guy she was going to marry wanted her to put me up for adoption, but she refused. I didn't know about the engagement until about a year ago, when I heard an elderly aunt talking about the breakup. When I questioned Becky, she teared up. I could see it still hurt. I want her to find love and I've listened to the way Rocky and Becky talk to one another. There's something there, Cherie. Maybe not love yet, but there's definitely something special going on between them. They are both lonely but would never admit it. They need our help."

"I don't see how we can make them fall for one another."

"Maybe they already have."

"Not a chance."

"No? Try seeing with your ears instead of your eyes. I

recognize it every time they're together. It's in their voice, the tender way they respond to one another."

"I won't dispute that it would be fantastic if it should happen. I'm willing to do whatever I can to push it in that direction, but frankly, I think it will take more than the two of us." She laughed. "We'll need a little help from the good Lord to pull it off."

"You've admitted it's peculiar how your daddy wound up here and even more peculiar that he'd invest in a business he's never shown an interest in before. Maybe it's too soon, but with a little help in the romance department, who can say what might happen? He's single. She's single. He's handsome, she's beautiful. Why not? I know Becky is fond of Rocky, and I think it's mutual."

"Yeah, but fondness isn't enough. I'm fond of Mr. Henry, but I don't want to marry him."

Angel stuck her finger down her throat and gagged. "Oooh, poor Mr. Henry. I don't need eyes to know when he walks in. I can smell him when he opens the door. Now, that man needs a wife."

Cherie laughed. "Maybe. But who would we wish him on?"

****

Rocky awoke at five-thirty, dressed and tiptoed through the apartment to keep from waking the girls, only to find them lying outside on quilts spread on the ground. He went into the café and motioned for Becky to go with him outside.

She shook her head and laughed, seeing the two girls sound asleep. "The Lord has answered my prayer."

"You prayed for them to sleep on the ground? I wish I had thought to pray the same thing around ten o'clock last night. I've never heard such racket."

"No, silly. But I've been praying for Angel to have a close friend. She has so many acquaintances, but she's never had a real friend."

"That's hard to believe. She's smart and has a terrific sense of humor. It's easy to forget that she's blind, she acts so normal."

"I agree, but I think therein lies the problem. Angel *is* normal. Being blind is not the issue. Feeling alone is the handicap. All of her acquaintances from school are blind, but most have been coddled and aren't as independent as Angel. You can't imagine how it did my heart good to hear the girls pleading to spend the night together."

"I'm delighted that they're having such a great time being with one another, but just a word of caution."

"What?"

"Next time they insist on a slumber party, it will be at your house. They giggled so loud, I finally had to go in and put a stop to it. I didn't get a wink of sleep until after two a.m. I suppose that's when they decided to sleep outside."

"Aww, that's so sweet. I love it."

"Sweet? I was ready to take a broom to them."

"Don't you see? That's the way it should be. I remember me and my friend Shera doing the same thing and how upset my mother would be when she'd storm into my room and dare us to say another word. Those are precious memories to look back on. Now, Angel will have that special memory of her and her best friend keeping you awake."

He rolled his eyes. "Women! I'll never understand them."

****

The flight to Miami was exciting, and for the first time since being released from the hospital, Lilah felt normal. The questions that plagued her for weeks seemed to vanish along with the clouds. When they arrived, a bus was waiting for them and transported them to the most beautiful hotel she'd ever seen.

The driver took care of their bags, and Coot took her by the hand and walked her into a gorgeous lobby. Looking around, she had no doubt that it was a very expensive place to stay. So, were they rich? After registering, Coot said, "We're on the eleventh floor. The manager says we each have a deck overlooking the city."

"Each?" When he didn't respond, she assumed she had misunderstood. But when the bell boy opened the door to the room and walked them in, he explained it was a suite, and the other room was separated by a bathroom. Coot asked him to place Lilah's luggage in the adjoining room.

After the young man left, Lilah said, "Did you know there would be two rooms?"

"Naturally."

"I don't understand. Coot, I don't know how to ask this any

other way, but is there a reason why you don't want to share a room with me?"

"Of course there's a reason. I'm concerned about your health."

"I still don't understand. It's not as if sharing a bed will somehow make me ill. Why don't you want to sleep with me?"

"Lilah, there you go again trying to find something to worry about. It's not that I don't want to. I don't need to."

"That doesn't make me feel any better. Were things this way before?"

"Before? So, you want to talk about the past. Why can't you forget the past?"

"I'm sorry, but this is not what I expected."

"What *did* you expect?"

"You referred to this trip as our honeymoon cruise. I guess I expected you to react as if we were newlyweds."

"It's too soon."

"Too soon? What does that mean? Did you book two rooms for the cruise, too?"

"I did and for a very good reason. If you don't trust my judgment, tell me, now."

"Oh, Coot, I know you're afraid if I get upset, I'll do something stupid again, but I've learned my lesson."

"I hope so. I love you, Lilah, and I was crushed when I discovered you no longer wanted to live. Then when you stayed in the coma so long, I was afraid you'd never wake up. I made a vow to myself that I would do anything to protect you. I couldn't stand it if you ever were to do something like that again." He threw up his hands. "There we go, dredging up the past. It's my duty to protect you, Lilah, and the way to do that is to move forward, not backward."

"Coot, I don't want you to feel you need to handle me with kid gloves. I won't break."

"But you did break, Lilah. If not for the nervous breakdown, you wouldn't have made the attempt on your life."

"What attempt? Nervous breakdown? Are you saying the virus didn't cause the coma? That it was somehow my fault?"

"Of course not. You misunderstood." He took her by the hand and walked over to the window. "Look at this gorgeous view. Have you ever seen so many city lights?"

Lilah wrapped her arm around his waist. "It is something to see, isn't it?"

Looking up she caught the sight of a tear in the corner of his eye. "Coot? You're crying."

His lip trembled. "If I am, it's happy tears. It's getting late. Why don't you go to your room, get on your gown and crawl under the covers for a good night's sleep. We set sail early." He pecked her on the forehead. "Goodnight, sweetheart."

"Goodnight, Coot."

Coot tossed and turned in his bed, but no way could he go to sleep. He'd always prided himself on being level-headed. Had he completely lost his mind? The woman in the next room belonged to another man. She and Rocky had already split up, and if he'd left things alone, there was a good chance she would be filing for divorce, and he might have a chance with her. But now—

He groaned. He might not be in this mess if Dovie Albertson hadn't convinced him that Lilah was in love with him and not with her husband. She lied. But why blame her? It didn't take much encouragement for him to go along with the crazy scheme until he found himself knee deep in his own little white lies.

Maybe he tried to fool himself into believing he hadn't outright lied, but there was no denying that he purposely skirted the truth to mislead Lilah into thinking they were married. It seemed harmless at the time. Almost as if he were involved in a game of make-believe. It was called 'play-like' when he was a child. He'd tell his sister, "Let's 'plyke' you're Dale Evans and I'm Roy Rogers." But he was no longer a kid and too old to play like he was married to the beautiful Lilah Albertson.

Forced to face the truth, he felt sick inside. She wasn't Lilah Albertson. She was Lilah Stone, wife of his former best friend, Rocky Stone. Had he completely lost his mind? Sure, he wanted her. He wanted her more than he'd ever wanted anyone or anything. He'd been willing to give up his practice for her. He'd still give up everything he owned to walk into that room, hold her in his arms and to have her as his own. But she wasn't his. She still belonged to Rocky.

Was it time to tell her the truth? Or should he wait until they returned home? Once she discovered she was lured on the ship under false pretenses, she'd never speak to him again. He wouldn't blame her.

When Lilah was first brought into the clinic, Coot had questioned how she could've ever thought suicide was a good idea. He now understood for the first time how someone could feel so hopeless that death would appear to be the only way out. He supposed the first question one would ask would be, "What do I have to live for?" He'd lost his position at Vanderbilt and let his nurse at the clinic go. He had no wife and no life. He pulled the pillow over his head and thought how nice it would be if he accidentally smothered in his sleep.

The ship set sail on time, and seeing the joy on Lilah's face almost made Coot forget what a louse he was. She was happy, but it would soon come to an end. What made him think he could pull off such an insane stunt? Stunt? It was no stunt. It was a criminal act. How else could it be described?

Lilah wanted to walk around the deck that evening, but he made excuses, saying she'd had enough excitement for the day. He told her they'd have ample time in the morning, and she should get some rest.

He retired to his own cabin, but tossed and turned until after three a.m. Then, with the sun shining in the portholes, he awoke with Lilah pouncing on the bed beside him, wearing a beautiful pink gown and negligee. She rolled over on the bed and kissed him.

Giggling, she said, "Good morning, sleepyhead."

He swallowed hard. "Lilah, go get dressed."

She sat up and frowned. "Who came in and stole your smile, you ol' grouch?"

"Sorry, I didn't get much sleep last night. Seriously, get dressed and let's go eat."

"Coot, talk to me. I know there's something troubling you. I sense that you're angry with me, but I don't know what I've done."

"How could I ever be angry with you. I love you. In fact, I love you too much."

She laughed. "How can a man love his wife too much?"

Coot sat upright. "Please, Lilah. Go dress."

After she left for her room, Coot sat on the edge of the bed with his face buried in his hands. He could either tell her the truth now, wait until they returned. . . or hope he could hide the truth forever. He was only fooling himself into believing the third scenario was a valid option.

After breakfast Coot and Lilah took their coffee on the deck. "Coot, how do you know you're in love with me?"

His brow lifted. "What prompted that peculiar question?"

She paused. "I don't want this to come out wrong or for you to misunderstand what I'm about to say, but—"

"I promise not to get upset. Say whatever you're thinking."

"Coot, any woman would be crazy not to fall in love with you. But—" She clamped her lips together. "Forget it. I don't know how to explain."

"Try. You've managed to start, so make an effort to finish."

"Well, I want that warm and fuzzy feeling that I must've felt when I married you. I've tried to bring it back. Do you suppose—" She clenched her eyes shut. "Oh, no. I see from your expression that I've hurt you, and that wasn't my intent."

"I know, but it's important you say how you feel. Go ahead, I'm listening."

"Thank you. I'm sure I must've been head-over-heels in love with you to want to marry you and I want to feel that way toward you again. I do. I thought if we came on this trip and were intimate again, maybe those romantic feelings would return. For your sake, I want to be a wife to you in every sense of the word."

He lowered his head. "For my sake?"

She reached over and caressed his cheek with her hand. "Oh, I knew this would happen. I've hurt you. Coot, I love you. I do. I'm just not *in* love with you, but I'm confident that given time, that will change. I'll grow to love you again. I will, because you deserve to be loved."

"Yes, Lilah, I love you than a man should love a woman. Especially if she is—" He wasn't ready to say it.

"Finish your statement. If she's what?"

"If she's not in love with him." He feigned a smile and stood.

"That isn't what you were going to say, is it?"

He reached for her hand. "Why don't we take a walk around the deck?" He had come close to telling her the truth. Maybe it was time he did.

While leaning on the rails, admiring the full moon, a little tow-headed boy walked over holding an ice cream cone. Coot pulled a handkerchief from his pocket and wiped his sticky little hands. "That looks quite good. What flavor?"

"Nilla."

His dad walked up behind them. "No, buddy, it's not vanilla. Don't you remember?"

Looking up at his father, he beamed. "Rocky!"

Lilah said, "What did you say?"

The kid said, "It's Rocky ice cream. Right, Daddy?"

"That's close, buddy. Rocky Road."

Lilah whispered. "Did he say Rocky?"

CHAPTER 21

"Coot, could we get a cone of ice cream?"

"Are you hungry?"

"Not really. But I want to try the flavor the kid was eating. Perhaps if I tasted it . . . oh, I suppose it's crazy, but I feel as if a memory is struggling to emerge. If only I could reach in my brain and pull it out."

"Lilah, we need to talk."

Smiling, she said, "I thought that's what we were doing."

"No, I mean really talk. There's something I need to tell you. Something I should've told you from the beginning."

"The beginning of what? Why are you sounding so mysterious, Coot?"

"Maybe mysterious is a good way to put it because it's a mystery to me how I could've gone along with such an insane plot."

"Ooh, so you're involved in a plot, are you?" She laughed. "I love a good mystery." Raising a brow, she giggled. "I do, don't I?

Love a good mystery?"

He mumbled, "I'm afraid you won't love this one. Let's go to our suite."

"What about the ice cream?"

"I don't think you'll want it when I finish telling you what I should've told you before coming on this cruise."

****

Cherie had always been a sucker for Second Chance Romance stories, and although Angel's plan wouldn't be easy to pull off, she agreed it was worth a try.

The girls plotted ways to get the love affair to blossom, and although some of their ideas fell flat, there were a few times when their little scheme worked even better than they anticipated. Yet, they still had a big job ahead of them and were running out of ideas.

Cherie commented that she had gone on youth trips with her church, and the pastor would have them to sit around the bonfire for a bonding time. She said, "I've never been to a bonfire when I didn't fall in love with some boy there."

Angel giggled. "Then, we definitely need a bonfire."

Cherie drew a picture on two notecards of four people roasting marshmallows on a starry night. Inside, she wrote an inscription, inviting Becky and Rocky to a special bonfire celebration.

The girls put the invitations on the counter near the cash register and waited for the recipients to find them. It was in the middle of the breakfast hour when Rocky walked up to the register, picked up the envelopes and held them up. When Becky walked by, he said, "What's this?"

"Where did you get it?"

"Sitting there next to the register." He opened his first, then let out a soft chuckle.

Becky glared, then reached for hers. "A wiener roast and marshmallow roasting party? It says it's a celebration. What are we celebrating?"

"He lifted his shoulders. Beats me! It's too late for Independence Day and too soon for Halloween. I wonder what they're up to."

"I have a pretty good idea," After the customers cleared out, Rocky walked over and picked up the invitation. "I wonder why they want us old fogies to join them? I have a feeling those girls of ours are up to something."

"I can guarantee it. Angel thinks she's very subtle but she's about as subtle as a rooster at sunup." Becky explained how her little sister was a romantic and had fears that she would wind up an old maid. "I was engaged once, but he broke it off whenever I became Angel's guardian."

"I'm sorry."

"Don't be. I'm not. It was fortunate that he let me know before the wedding that he wanted me to put Angel up for adoption."

"Did you love him?"

"I did. But I have no regrets. I made the right decision. But

Angel heard Memaw's sister talk about what a pity it was that I was saddled down with a handicapped child. Since then, Angel has wanted me to find true love."

Rocky said, "That's cute. I've just thought of something." He suggested that he and Becky go along with their little scheme and pretend to fall in love. "The joke will be on them."

Becky cackled out loud. "That will be hilarious. Let's do it."

Later that afternoon Becky thanked Angel for the invitation and told her she and Rocky looked forward to going. "It sounds like fun, and we both agreed it would be nice if more people could join us."

Angel smiled. "Maybe next time."

Becky clasped her hands together. "Ah, but I have a surprise. Miss Annie and Miss Reba's twin nephews are coming to Kennesaw for a visit tomorrow, and I told the sisters you girls would love having the boys join us."

"Aww, Becky, that's not a good idea. We don't know them."

"What better way to get acquainted than around a campfire?"

Angel jumped up. "I need to run over and see Cherie."

"You just saw her fifteen minutes ago."

"I know, but I need to tell her about the boys. Becky, you should've talked with me first. We wanted it to be cozy. You know, just the four of us?"

"I'm sorry, honey. But a party sounded like so much fun, I thought it would be a shame not to share it. Then, when Miss Reba said their nephews would be visiting, I thought you girls would be excited."

****

Friday morning Cherie and Angel were busy helping out in the café and had very little time to talk about the plan.

When Cherie waited on the Duvall sisters, Miss Annie said, "I told our nephews that they had a special invitation to a party, given by two beautiful young ladies."

Cherie's mouth hurt when she attempted to smile. "Yes ma'am." She hoped they'd drop the subject. Her knees felt weak, and her stomach tied in knots as she glanced from one old-maid to the other. She began to hyperventilate at the mental picture of cross-eyed twin boys with big ears, big noses, and high-pitched, squeaky voices. This was one time that Angel would have an advantage. She could pretend they were good-looking.

Angel walked over and whispered. "Are you dressing up tonight?"

"No. Why should I? The boys will probably come wearing overalls."

"Then I'll wear my dungarees. If we dressed up, it would probably make them uncomfortable."

"Not as uncomfortable as I'm gonna be with them sitting there."

****

The afternoon of the party, Rocky built a big fire between the back of the garage apartment and the woods. The first week in August in Alabama seemed a bad time to plan a bonfire, yet he found himself feeling like a school kid. He brought the lawn furniture from around front. A glider and four chairs. Perfect. It had been a long time since he'd done anything fun and plotting this with Becky made it twice as much fun. They'd put on a real show for the girls.

Becky said when the girls were convinced there was something going on between them, they'd suggest playing Penny. She said, "We'll go walking, and when we come out of the woods, we'll be holding hands and looking all lovey-dovey. Then, after they're convinced their plan worked, we'll yell, 'Gotcha,' and let them know they weren't as subtle as they thought."

He hoped he could pull it off without laughing. It had been a long time since he played Penny, and the last time he did, he wound up marrying the girl he walked with.

****

The invitations stated that the party would begin at eight o'clock. The girls agreed it was important that it be dark. Too excited to wait, the girls were outside, checking out the setting an hour early. Cherie said, "We need to pull the chairs closer to the fire. The glow from the light will be flattering on their faces."

Angel laughed, "Not to mention how hot it will be, which should be an incentive for them to get up and walk together. If we're lucky, the heat will make the boys decide to leave early."

Cherub groaned. "It's going to be so weird having them here. We'll have to talk to them, but it'll be awkward, since we have nothing in common."

"I feel the same way. I know Becky meant well, but she should've consulted us before inviting others to our party."

Rocky walked up at seven-forty-five. "Isn't it about time for the party to begin?"

Cherie's mouth gaped open.

"What's wrong, honey?"

"Wow! Just wow! You look . . . you look very handsome tonight, Daddy."

"Tonight? Are you saying I'm not always handsome?"

"Of course you are. Aren't those new slacks?"

"I've had them for a good while. Just never had a place to wear them. Too dressy for the café, and too casual for church. If you think they're inappropriate, I'll go put on blue jeans."

"No! They're perfect. I mean they'll do fine. Don't change. That white shirt shows off your tan. And your muscles."

"I grew the muscles especially for the party. I'm glad you approve, honey."

"That's cute, Daddy. A sense of humor makes you seem younger. Not like an old fuddy duddy."

Angel whispered, "I have a feeling this is going to be a perfect night."

Rocky kept looking next door, wondering how much longer before Becky would arrive.

He said, "Not that you both aren't cute as buttons, but isn't it time you girls dressed for the party?"

Cherub said, "Did I fail to mention it's a 'Come as you are, party?'"

"I believe you did."

"Oh, sorry. Don't worry about it. You look great, Daddy."

Angel said, "Becky was taking a bath when I left the house. She should be here shortly."

Cherie had her back turned when her daddy let out a cat whistle. Her eyes widened when she whirled around and saw Becky walking toward him. Cherie ran over and whispered to Angel. "Your sister looks like a movie star, and you should see the look on my Daddy's face. He's devouring her with his eyes."

"This may be easier than we thought. What is she wearing?"

Cherie described the pink gingham spaghetti strap dress, and the rose in her hair. "I can tell he's smitten. but what man wouldn't be. She's gorgeous. From the way Daddy whistled, and the way Becky blushed, I wouldn't be surprised if you and I aren't calling each other 'sister' before next Christmas."

Angel smiled when she heard Rocky tell Becky she looked beautiful, and it was easy to discern from her sister's voice that she was flattered. Maybe Rocky and Becky didn't need help. She turned when Cherie pulled on her shirt and whispered. "Uh-oh! The twins are here."

Angel let out a groan. "Ugh. I was hoping they'd forget."

"Oh, my!"

"What's wrong, Cherie?"

"You know how we worried that Miss Reba would drive the boys over and stay for the Party? Well, that's not gonna happen."

"Did Miss Annie bring them? I thought she lost her license."

"Angel, they drove themselves . . . in a new Thunderbird. A beautiful, shiny red Thunderbird." She stopped and bit her tongue. "I'm sorry. I wasn't thinking. You have no idea what a Thunderbird looks like."

"You're right, but I don't care about the car. What do the twins look like."

Cherie's heart beat like a jackhammer. "Like two young Paul Newman's. I know that doesn't tell you much either, but they're even better looking than Tip Olds."

Angel laughed. "Thanks, that helps. Now, I get the picture," she giggled. "Maybe we should've dressed, after all."

"Yikes. I forgot. Oh, I wish I had taken time to brush my hair and dress."

Angel said, "Too late, now. Let's go welcome them." They hurried toward their guests. Cherie told them how she and Angel had looked forward to getting acquainted. She quickly explained that she and Angel had been busy and hadn't had time to dress, but it would only take a minute. She took Angel by the hand, and they hurried up the steps to the apartment. Cherie pulled out two of her best dresses, brushed her hair, while Angel dressed and pulled her hair a ponytail.

They scurried back to the party and found the boys chatting with Rocky as they roasted wieners on bent coat hangers over the open fire.

The four teenagers were having such a great time getting acquainted, the girls almost forgot the plan was to help Rocky and Becky find love. Cherie said, "Daddy, why don't you and Becky have a seat in the glider and enjoy the fire?"

"It's a party, sweetheart, and I have a better idea. Why don't we play a game of Penny?"

Becky said, "What a fun idea. I haven't played Penny since high school."

Billy said, "Y'all know how to play Penny? I didn't know they played it back in your day."

Rocky laughed. "My generation invented the game and I'm still not too old to enjoy a moonlight walk with a beautiful girl." He turned to Becky and said, "Why don't we start it off and show these kids how it's done?"

Angel said, "I don't know how to play." Cherub assured her it was so easy, even a blind person could do it. "Everyone puts their palms together, as if preparing to pray. Daddy will slip his penny into a girl's hand, and then he'll say, 'Penny, penny, who's got the penny.' Becky will slip her penny into a guy's hands. Then Daddy and Becky will leave for a walk, and the game keeps on going until everyone has had a chance to go walking."

Becky said, "It really is a great way to get acquainted at a party, but we may not have enough people here for it to work."

The twins said, in unison, "We have enough to play. Let's do it."

Rocky's eyes squinted. The fellows appeared a bit too eager. Maybe this wasn't such a great idea, after all. Too late now, to back out. He gave his penny to Angel and Becky gave hers to Bobby, who had been eyeing Becky's little sister from the time they first arrived.

Becky whispered in Bobby's ear. "She's blind."

"Yes ma'am. Aunt Reba told me. I'll hold her hand when we walk to make sure she doesn't stumble on something." He walked over and whispered to Angel. "My brother is at three o'clock. Hold out the penny when you smell Old Spice, and I'm sure he'll see to it that it drops into his hands." He chuckled. "Aunt Annie told us there were two pretty girls over here, and my aunt doesn't lie. I think Billy took a bath in the aftershave." Angel laughed. "You're funny."

"And you are beautiful. Thank you for inviting us." He was full of questions and Angel had never felt so comfortable around someone she had just met. He wanted to know how long she'd be staying in Kennesaw, and he seemed pleased to learn she'd be there all summer. He asked if she'd mind if he called on her while he was visiting his aunts.

"I thought you and your brother were leaving Sunday."

"I think we've had a change of plans."

Angel couldn't separate the emotions stirring within her heart.

He was the first seeing boy to ever show an interest in her, but was he really interested or was it pity he felt? She didn't want his sympathy.

After walking around the block, Angel and Bobby got back to the bonfire only minutes before Billy and Cherie. When they walked up, Angel could tell by Cherie's voice that she was enjoying Billy's company. But what happened to Rocky and Becky?

The kids were standing around the fire, roasting marshmallows when Rocky and Becky finally walked out of the woods, holding hands. They sat together in the glider. Close together.

Cherie whispered to Angel. "They came out of the woods holding hands, and Becky has her head on Daddy's shoulder. They're looking up at the stars."

"For real? You aren't joking?"

"Nope. Not only that, Becky had her hair pulled up in a twist when they left, and now it's down over her shoulders. And . . . she's holding the flower she had pinned in her hair when they went on the walk."

"That seems strange, doesn't it? It sounds like things are moving way too fast."

"That's what I was wondering. Maybe they've been hiding their feelings from us. You think?"

"I don't know what to think."

Bobby said, "Mr. Stone, that was a fun game. Would you

mind if we play again? This time Angel and I will go first."

Becky smiled. "We really need more to play."

Billy jumped up and grabbed Cherub's hand. "We have enough. I don't mind. Do you?"

Cherie's smile lit up her face. "Nope. Let's go."

Rocky squirmed. The brazen kid was moving a bit too fast. How old was he, anyway? "Hold on, Cherie. You haven't been given the penny yet."

Bobby flipped the coin to Rocky and laughed. "They don't need it. Stick it back in your pocket and take your lady friend for a moonlight stroll. See you later, alligator."

The kids went running off into the night and Becky said, "My feet are killing me. I shouldn't have worn these heels. Would you mind if we sat this one out?"

"This one? I plan for it to be the last one. I'm not too keen on the girls running off into the woods with two men I don't know from Adam."

Fifteen minutes later, Rocky looked at his watch. "They've been gone a long time. Maybe I should go check on them."

"They're fine, Rocky. Billy and Bobby seem like very sweet boys."

"Boys? Are you kidding? They're fully grown men with a five o'clock shadow."

"They're eighteen and the girls are sixteen. Stop worrying."

CHAPTER 22

The ladies in the Women's Quarterly Meeting group, had been taking turns fixing meals for their dear friend, Dovie, since her stroke. Some said it was brought on by a delusion that her daughter was off on some imaginary cruise and would be returning home soon.

Hazel stayed with her every night. According to the doctor from Hartford, her biggest problem was not the paralysis, but a shattered heart.

He said, "She seems intent on punishing herself." He encouraged Hazel to let her talk about Lilah and Cherub as much as she needed to. Hazel did as the doctor requested, although she felt it was a mistake. Dovie had nothing else on her mind and repeated the same regrets over and over. How many times had she said, "If I could just have one more chance, I'd do things differently." If Hazel didn't ask, she'd invariably say, "Don't you want to know what I'd do differently?"

Then forced to nod, Dovie took it as her cue to start from the beginning. Hazel was sure it hadn't all taken place the way Dovie repeated each time. They'd been friends since high school, almost sixty years ago, and in all that time, she'd never known Dovie to be as vindictive as she now seemed to want everyone to believe. It was almost an obsession with her. Tonight was no different.

Hazel handed her a washbowl with a little soap and water and a washcloth. "When you finish, I'll help you into a clean gown."

Dovie said, "Hazel, I don't know why you're so good to me. I'm nothing but a sorry, no-account ol' woman whose main objective in life has been to make those I love the most, most miserable."

Hazel wanted to say, "Stop it," but recalling the doctor's words, she sat back and waited for what she knew was coming next.

"I've destroyed the lives of the people who loved me best and managed to fool those who know me the least. You and I have been friends a long time, but you don't know me Hazel. If you did, you wouldn't give me the time of day."

"That's not true, Dovie. We all have our bad days. Goodness, Luther can tell you, I have my share."

"You also have three sons, a daughter, and how many grandchildren?"

Beaming, Hazel said, "Eight, soon to be nine."

Dovie said, "And they all sat around your table on Mother's

Day. Am I right?"

"Absolutely. Did I tell you about the bouquet the grandkids picked for me out of my yard? Roger scolded them, but I told him not to be so hard on them. I thought it was so sweet of—".

Dovie cut her off. "See what I mean? You're a good woman. I appreciated the plate full of food you sent to me. It was delicious, but food wasn't what I needed."

"What did you need?"

"Forgiveness. I was alone on Mother's Day, and I knew it was my own doing."

Hazel said, "Dovie, you're too hard on yourself. You know Lilah would've been with you if she could have. I know losing her has been awful for you."

"I've lost her alright, but she could come back if she wanted to. She doesn't want to, and I have no one to blame but myself."

"Dovie, you aren't thinking straight. You've convinced yourself that she's on a cruise—shucks, you even had me convinced for a while—but your Lilah has gone to Heaven. And as much as she loved you—and I know she did—she wouldn't want to come back."

Dovie grabbed her hand. Her eyes had a look of desperation. "Hazel, I've done an awful thing. If it weren't for me, my Lilah would still be with the only man she's ever truly loved, and sweet-little Cherub would be happy. She loves them both."

"Dovie, don't torture yourself with thoughts of what might have been. Life is filled with heartaches and disappointments. I wish things were different for you. It hurts me to see you so despondent, but there are some things in life we must accept."

Dovie supposed those words were meant to be comforting, but Hazel couldn't possibly understand. Easy for her to say. She had a family who loved her.

****

Rocky kept glancing at his watch. Was Becky really so naïve she didn't know how dangerous it could be to send two pretty little girls out into the night with two brutes who looked as if they might've completed the Charles Atlas course? He saw the way those hoodlums gobbled up Cherub and Angel with their eyes. They were practically salivating. The girls had both been sheltered. They wouldn't see it coming. He jumped up. "I'm going to see what's going on. They should be back by now."

Becky laughed. "Sit back down, Rocky. You might as well get used to this. Your baby girl is growing up. Trust her."

"It's not her I don't trust. It's those young scalawags." What was the purpose in having a bonfire if they were going to spend so much time away? He supposed Becky could be right and he was allowing his imagination to run on overtime, but he'd feel much better if the girls were sitting where he could keep an eye on them.

Becky whispered, "Here they come. Feel better, now?"

"Better?" Seeing his baby girl holding hands with a young man caused an ache in his gut. Cherie had never favored her mother as much as she did at that moment. Was it his imagination or did the twins favor Coot Culpepper? His teeth clenched. Would the hurt ever go away?

Billy and Bobby thanked Rocky and Becky for inviting them to the party and told the girls they would be hearing from them after returning home. Rocky managed to hold his tongue, when Cherub batted her long, thick lashes as she gazed up into the ol' boy's eyes, and said, "I had a great time, Billy. Don't forget to write."

Rocky glared at the six-foot brute. He recognized a look of longing when he saw it, and he definitely saw it. He wanted to punch him in the face, and if not for the fact he might lose his daughter if he did, he managed to restrain himself.

Becky's heart ached for Angel, knowing how much it must hurt to hear that Billy and Cherie would be keeping in touch through letters. She said, "I'm so glad you boys could come, and Bobby, if you and Angel would like to keep in touch, I'll make sure I read all your letters to her, and I'm pretty good at taking dictation."

Angel laughed. "She's kidding, Bobby. No way!"

Becky's brow furrowed. "Well, I hope there would be nothing in them, that either of you would be ashamed for me to see."

Bobby said, "No ma'am. But you probably wouldn't want Angel reading your letters from Mr. Rocky, either, although I'm sure there'd be nothing improper in them."

Angel giggled. "I think you'd better go, Bobby, while the

going is good."

"You're probably right. I had a wonderful time, Angel, and don't forget what I told you."

"Forget? I'll remember it forever. And don't lose my phone number."

"I have it memorized, already. Just sit by the phone every Friday night at six o'clock."

Becky glared at Bobby and shook her head. "Angel, honey, that's long distance. Writing is cheaper."

Bobby said, "But calling is cheaper than driving from Auburn, Alabama to Kennesaw every Friday. Although, I'll admit I'd much rather see her than to talk on the phone. But for a while, this will have to do."

Becky opened her mouth to object, but Cherub ran over and grabbed Angel's hand. "Come on, let's walk the guys to their car."

Rocky watched them as they rounded the corner of the café. He whispered to Becky. "Can you see them?"

Smiling she said, "No, but I think that was the idea."

"Keep me grounded, Becky. This is all new to me. I want Cherie to have a little freedom . . . just not too much freedom. I need help in knowing where to draw the line."

"They're normal teenagers, Rocky, and they're having a good time. That makes me happy."

"Me too. But Cherie and Angel aren't the only ones who enjoyed tonight."

"You're right. Billy and Bobby seemed quite taken with the girls, didn't they?"

Rocky reached over and turned her face toward him. "I wasn't referring to the boys." He leaned forward until their lips met. Then, as if someone had lit a firecracker under him, he jumped up. "I'm sorry. I'm so sorry, Becky. I don't know what came over me." He paced back and forth in circles, running his hand through his hair. "I didn't plan to do that. I promise."

She looked up and smiled. "Was I complaining? Sit back down. We need to talk."

His mind reeled. Was she going to tell him she couldn't work for someone who would take advantage of her? His heart felt as if an ape was sitting on his chest.

"Rocky, I know you aren't in love with me, so I don't want you to feel embarrassed or shamed because we allowed the moonlight to arouse romantic feelings in us."

"Us?"

Smiling, she said, "Yes. I wanted you to kiss me, even though I knew it was the bonfire, the stars, the moon, and the handsome guy sitting so close he made my heart go pitter-patter. It's a feeling I haven't had in a long time. Truthfully, I hadn't expected to ever experience it again. I didn't fool myself into thinking it was love, but it gave me hope that I could still be capable of feeling love again."

"Thank you, Becky. You're one of a kind and a man would be out of his mind for not falling head over heels in love with you.

And if I wasn't a married man—"

"I thought your wife was dead?"

He lowered his head. "She is." Running his wedding band around on his left hand, his voice was so low he wasn't sure she heard him. "Becky, you are a beautiful woman . . . a very desirable woman, and I know what I'm about to say won't make sense to you. Shucks, I can't even understand it." He paused, biting his lower lip.

"Try me."

He nodded. "Lilah and I were not living together when she died. For all I know, she hated me. But until I can accept the fact that she's gone and begin to think of myself as being single, I won't be capable of loving another woman the way she deserves to be loved. I still think of myself as a married man."

"I understand."

"Do you?"

"I do. But Rocky, don't hold it against me when I tell you I fear I could easily find myself falling in love with you. For twelve years, I haven't longed to have a man kiss me. But tonight, I felt alive again."

"Oh, Becky, you deserve so much more. It was the mood tonight. We played the game, but I'm afraid we played it too well. I don't want to hurt you, but if I stay here, I'm afraid I might."

Her brow creased into a frown. "If you stay here? What are you saying?"

"You've been good for me, Becky. You've given me purpose."

"If I didn't know better, I'd think this was goodbye."

He reached for her hand. "When I left home, I was in a bad place, emotionally. Winding up on the road to Kennesaw that night was one of the best things that's ever happened to me. You and the café saved my life. It's time for me to go, Becky, but I want to deed the Sam & Sadie to you, and Angel."

"What? That's crazy."

"No, it isn't. Cherie and I will be heading back to Alabama. And as much as I detest being around her grandmother, there's no doubt in my mind that Dovie loves Cherie, and Lilah wouldn't want me to shut her mother out of Cherie's life. That relationship needs to be restored."

"You don't know what you're saying, Rocky."

"I do. Before coming here, I sold a few acres of land that wasn't fit for much of anything. But I made more money off that piece of property than I ever dreamed of having. I can afford to do this. You've made the café what it is today, and you deserve to own it."

Tears trailed down her cheeks. "Rocky, do you realize how offensive that sounds to me?"

"Offensive?"

"Yes. I tell you I wanted you to kiss me, and you immediately want to buy me off and leave town?"

"That's crazy. I wasn't buying you off. I'm nuts about you

Becky, and if I could get over this feeling of being unfaithful to Lilah, I'd ask you to marry me tonight. I want to love you and take care of you, but it would be unfair for me to ask you, until I can let go of Lilah."

"Rocky, I would never expect you to forget her. When Tim left me, I thought I'd never love again, and until you came along, I hadn't met a man who could turn my head. But then you showed up, and you were so gentle and kind." She winked. "I won't deny that being breathtakingly handsome didn't enter into the equation, but I knew from the start you were different. Then, when we went walking, the mood was set, and I longed for you to hold me. Rocky, I don't know what transpired tonight, but I've discovered my heart is indeed big enough to love again. I know yours is, too. You felt something tonight. I know you did."

"You're right. I did. And it scared me to death."

"Why? We did nothing wrong."

CHAPTER 23

Rocky told Cherie to go upstairs, and he'd be up as soon as he made sure the bonfire was out. Sitting alone, he groaned at the mess he'd made of his life.

Not only his own life, but his actions ruined the lives of everyone around him. Perhaps if he'd been more understanding toward Dovie, he could've learned to love her the way Lilah did. Surely, he could've found something in the woman to admire. But he was young and impatient when he and Lilah married and instead of sitting down and talking things out with his mother-in-law, he chose to make her life as miserable as she was making his. What if he'd been kinder? How could he be sure she wouldn't have chosen to go back home if she'd felt her daughter was married to a nice guy? Why couldn't he understand at the time, the stress put on Lilah by insisting she turn her back on her mother?

Too late now. Or was it? He couldn't bring Lilah back, but wasn't he doing the same thing with Cherub? Didn't she feel she had to choose to love him or love her grandmother? Rocky did something he hadn't done in a long time. He prayed for the Lord to take away the hate he'd harbored toward Dovie, and to help him forgive. Before he finished the prayer, he discovered a miracle had taken place. God removed the anger before he asked, and he hadn't realized it until now.

Cherie walked out on the porch of the garage apartment, and yelled, "Daddy, what are you doing?"

He looked up. "I'm coming sweetheart." After stomping out the last live embers, he headed up the stairs. He put his arm around his daughter. "Pack your bags, sweetheart. We're leaving."

"Leaving? Where?"

"We're going home."

"But we are home."

"No. Our home is in Nearby."

Giant tears flowed down her cheeks. Rocky assumed it was happy tears, until the squalling began.

"You can't do this to me, Daddy."

"What are you talking about? I'm sure you miss your grandmother, and I know she misses you."

"So, you planned all along to take me back and drop me off? What have I done?"

"Oh, honey, I'm not dropping you off. I'm going back, too."

"That's crazy."

"No, sweetheart. I'm finally doing something that makes

sense."

"Well, I'm not going."

Rocky stood with his mouth gaping open. This was certainly not the reaction he expected. "Okay, sit down and tell me what's bothering you." He bit his lip, imagining that he'd said exactly what Lilah would've wanted him to say. Too many times, in the past, he'd been too slow to listen to the opinions of others.

Cherub flopped down in the chair with her arms folded across her midsection. "I'll go live with Becky and Angel. They'll let me. I know they will."

"Honey, I love Becky and Angel, also, but they aren't family. We need to go make amends with your grandmother."

"Who are you trying to kid? You hate her and she hates you."

"Hate is a very strong word. I don't hate Dovie, although I may have acted like it at times. How can I hate a woman who brought such a wonderful daughter into the world and trained her to be the loving, Christian woman that I learned to love?"

"Daddy, are you sure you're alright? You're talking crazy."

"No, I'm finally making sense, Cherie."

"Well, you can go, and you and Big Mama can love on each other if that's what you expect to happen. Besides, Billy thinks he and Bobby may get to stay a couple more days."

"Sweetheart, those boys are going off to college soon, and you and Angel will likely never see them again. There'll be other boys. What about that Olds boy in Nearby?"

"That's exactly what he is . . . a boy! Sure, I had a crush on him once, but that was all."

"All? What else would it be?" For a fleeting moment, he wished he hadn't asked.

Looking at him as if he had spaghetti for brains, she said, "Love?"

"Well, there'll be plenty of time for that later. Be patient."

"Daddy, don't you understand? I'm already in love, and Billy loves me. If I move to Nearby, we'll never see one another again. He says he'll come visit his aunts every chance he gets, so I'll at least see him on holidays and summer vacation."

"Honey, you've only seen the guy one time. You can't possibly be in love."

She burst into tears. "I knew you wouldn't understand. Mama would've believed me. She believed in love at first sight. She once told me that she remembered the first time she laid eyes on you—that you were wearing a blue plaid shirt and you walked into the principal's office to register for school. She said you both were going into ninth grade."

"She said *that*?"

"She sure did. You don't remember seeing her when you first moved to Nearby?"

"Of course I remember. I just didn't know she noticed me. I walked into the office, and she was in there sharpening a pencil. She was the prettiest girl I'd ever seen in my life, but I didn't know she noticed me. She never told me."

"Did you tell her?"

"No."

"Well, I believe one should say how they feel. Although I didn't tell Billy I loved him until after he told me, I would've admitted it before the night was over. I believe in being honest with one another. Haven't you tried to teach me that honesty is the best policy?"

Rocky hoped his thoughts weren't written on his face. The idea of that brute feeding his little girl such a line made chills run up his spine. His head swam with questions he wanted to ask her about their walk, but he had sense enough to know he could blow it if the answers weren't the ones he wanted to hear.

Besides, Cherie would probably never see the guy again and Rocky had something else pressing on his mind. So, Lilah said it was love at first sight? He chewed the inside of his jaw, remembering the feeling he had at fifteen when he walked in the new school, and saw her. His knees got week, his stomach felt as if he'd swallowed a swarm of butterflies, and his heart thumped so loud he was afraid she'd hear it. She smiled and said, "You're new, aren't you?" He nodded and said, "uh-huh." He remembered lying in bed that night and thinking of a million brilliant things he wished he'd said, instead of acting like such a dunce.

If only he had known she loved him from the start, it could've saved him a lot of heartbreak, since he was always positive she preferred Coot Culpepper over him. Why wouldn't she? All the other girls did, and it was obvious Coot was sweet on her. Rocky thought back to their Senior year and how he longed to take her to the Homecoming Dance. He didn't ask, because he was sure she wanted Coot to ask her.

Cherie said, "Well, haven't you?"

"Haven't I what?"

"Where is your mind, Daddy? I said I believe in being honest and then I asked if it wasn't what you taught me to do?"

"Sure, honey. Honesty is the best policy." Rocky winced, after recapping the conversation. Sure, he wanted her to be honest, but did she have to be so eager?

CHAPTER 24

Coot was ruined. It was obvious, even to him, that only a deranged mind could've pulled such a stupid stunt, thinking they'd get away with it. Maybe if he'd used good judgment, he would've had a chance with Lilah—now that Rocky was out of the picture—but he'd ruined any hopes of a life with her. In a sixty-second span, he'd thought of sixty good reasons why he should forget about telling her the awful truth. It was no good. To think he could return to Nearby was a farce. He was done. He'd lost Lilah, lost his practice, and lost his reputation. And for what? To win? Wasn't that really how this all started, back in junior high?

Lilah reached for Coot's clammy palm and felt him pull away.

"Coot, are you in some kind of trouble?"

"Trouble? I will be when I tell you what I've done."

"You're scaring me."

"You're not nearly as scared as I am. I've done an awful thing." He sat for several seconds, staring into her big beautiful, innocent eyes. He had no choice but to take her back to Nearby, put her off at her mother's house, drive away and never look back.

Where would he go? Not back to Nashville. Dovie would set out to find him and that would be the first place she'd look.

Lilah said, "Please, Coot, tell me, whatever it is. It can't be that bad."

His chin trembled. "It's worse than you could ever imagine. I'd give anything if I didn't have to tell you."

"Why? I'm your wife. Right? You should be able to tell me anything."

"That's just it. You aren't my wife."

She sat for a second, allowing his words to sink in. "What are you saying, Coot?"

"I don't know where to start."

"Why not the beginning?"

"If I start at the beginning, it will look as if I'm putting it off on your mother, and that would be wrong." He lowered his head, unable to look at her. "Dovie wrote to me at the hospital in Nashville, saying you had confided in her that you'd always been in love with me."

Lilah shook her head. "I'm sorry, Coot, but that wasn't true."

"I know that now. But don't blame Dovie for the mistakes I've made. I've known all along what I was doing was wrong, but it was my obsession to win that drove me." He lifted his head and glared into her eyes. "Hold on. You said it wasn't true?"

"Because it wasn't."

"You're beginning to remember, aren't you?"

"Yes."

He covered his face with his hands. "Oh, Lilah, you must hate me."

"Coot, why don't you finish, and allow me to decide if I hate you."

"Trust me, you have every right. I hate myself for what I've done. Rocky Stone was my best friend growing up, but we were always very competitive."

She smiled. "I remember."

"You do?"

She nodded.

"Then you must recall that the competition was fierce. . . football, grades, popularity . . . everything. You were the prettiest girl in high school, and we aggressively competed for your affection. When you chose him, I was furious. However, I'm beginning to realize it had nothing to do with unrequited love. I was angry that I lost to Rocky."

He expected her to cry, scream, even slap him. But she calmly listened. Once he began, the whole sordid truth rolled off his tongue so fast he was admitting things he wasn't sure he was required to reveal.

"After you and Rocky married, the competition was over, and I put everything I had into becoming the best surgeon, I could be. That is, until I received your mother's letter. It was as if I suddenly reverted to my teenage years. I had a chance to win. I left a thriving practice, moved back and set out to make you fall in love with me."

"Even though you knew you didn't love me?"

"That's the thing. I didn't know. Lilah, I called it love. But once I had you all to myself, in my own home, I realized there was something missing. I won, but it wasn't the feeling of euphoria I expected. Although I've never really been in love, I knew this wasn't it. I loved you, but I wasn't in love with you. However, I had gone too far to turn back. Besides, I now had Dovie to contend with. She wanted us to be together, and I knew she had the potential to ruin me if I crossed her."

"Tell me, Coot. What did you plan to do after the cruise."

"I didn't know. I kept praying for a way to get out of the mess I was in, but I saw no way out." He wrung his hands. "Well, that's about it. If you still want a cone of Rocky Road ice cream, I'll go buy it for you."

"No."

"Lilah, I feel like such a heel, but I'm glad I no longer have to hide the truth from you. I would never have believed I could do something so low down . . . so deceitful, and especially to someone I care so much about."

She reached over and with the back of her hand, wiped his tears. "Coot, thank you."

"Did you not comprehend what I was saying. Why would you

thank me?"

"For being a great doctor, bringing me on this cruise, and helping me to recall my past."

"Oh, Lilah! I don't deserve such kindness. Don't you get it? I took advantage of your memory loss and pretended you were my wife."

"But you didn't. And you could have. You treated me as your patient, but never as your wife. You slept in a separate room when I was convalescing in your home. You rented a suite at the hotel and booked two staterooms on the cruise. You never once forgot, nor did you act as if I were anything more than a friend you cared for. I thank you for that, Coot."

"How long have you known?"

"I began to have flashbacks when I heard the kid say, 'Rocky ice cream'. but I wanted to wait and see how long it would take for you to fill in the gaps. I knew you would."

"How did you know?"

"I suddenly realized why we were sleeping in separate quarters. You're a good man, Coot, and I hope one day you find someone who loves you as deeply and sincerely as you're capable of loving. She'll be a blessed woman."

"Lilah, I don't know what to say. I wanted to tell you, shortly after the farce began, but I felt I had gone too far to back down. I didn't know how to stop it. The cruise was my way of running away until I could figure out a way to get out of the mess I had made. I closed the clinic. I didn't think I could ever show my face in Nearby again."

"Well, you'll open back up as soon as we get home."

"That would never work. Although you've forgiven me, there are others—namely, your mother and Rocky—who will want to run me out of town on a rail. I'll pack up and leave as quickly as possible after returning home."

"That would be a mistake. Nearby needs you. You've done nothing wrong. I'm the one who messed up. I was the reason Rocky left. It was all my fault."

"I find that hard to believe. Do you still love him?"

"With all my heart. I love him so much, I didn't want to live without him."

"Then let him know, Lilah."

"I plan to. The separation was all my fault."

"I can't believe that."

"But it's true. Coot, you've learned how controlling my mama can be. She lived with us and treated me as if I were her little girl. She was cruel to Rocky, but I couldn't stand up to her. Rocky asked me to choose him or Mama. I was too frightened to tell her to leave, so I told him if someone had to go it would be him. I knew Mama wouldn't leave and I believed Rocky loved me too much to go. I was wrong. He left."

"You weren't wrong, Lilah. Rocky loves you and you love him. It's time to put your marriage back together."

"I plan to. I can hardly wait to get home to see my husband

and my sweet daughter."

****

After arriving back in Nearby, Lilah said, "Drop me off at my cottage."

Coot's eyes widened. "I forgot. You don't know."

"Know what?"

"Rocky sold the cottage, and it's been torn down."

"What? Impossible. Rocky loves that place. He bought it just before we married. He wouldn't have sold it without talking it over with me. We both loved it."

"Lilah, he couldn't ask you. You were in a coma."

Her eyes watered. "Where is he staying?"

"I don't know, but he moved your mother and daughter to the farm."

"Then take me there."

Coot retrieved Lilah's luggage from the trunk of the car, then sat it on the porch. "I hope you won't hold it against me if I don't go in. I'm not ready to face Dovie. She's gonna be furious when she learns I've confessed our little sinister plot."

Lilah was stunned when Hazel Brown came walking into the living room, her mouth gaping open. She grabbed Lilah in a hug. "It's true! It's true!"

Lilah said, "Are you all right Mrs. Brown?"

"Oh, m'goodness, honey. Look at you." She held her out at arms length and laughed. "You are as much alive as I am. Your mother tried to tell us you weren't dead."

Lilah smiled, thinking how gossip tends to travel in small towns. "Didn't Mama tell you I went on a cruise to recuperate?"

"She told us about the cruise, but no one believed her."

Lilah thought it strange that folks would choose to believe a lie when the truth would fit better. "Where's Mama?"

"Sugar, your mama had a blood clot in her leg and has suffered a stroke. She's not doing

well. I've been staying with her. She'll be so glad to see you. The doctor from Hartford just left after giving her a shot of morphine."

"A stroke? And Cherie? Is she here?"

"No, she's with her daddy."

"That's good. Thank you, Mrs. Brown, but you can go now. I'll be here with Mama."

Lilah walked back to her mother's room. "Mama. I'm back."

Dovie opened her eyes and burst into full blown sobs. "Oh, Lilah, my baby. Come sit on the side of the bed. I'm dying, sugar, and I prayed the good Lord would give me the chance to tell you the truth, before He calls me home. Tell Coot to come in here. I want him to hear this, too. I've not only wronged you, I've wronged him. He's a good man, Lilah. Please don't blame him. It was all my fault."

"Coot went home, Mama, but I'm listening."

Lilah sat quietly as Dovie poured out her heart, admitting lies and evil deeds she committed in order to get Rocky out of Lilah's life, and to replace him with Coot. Though much of what she said coincided with Coot's version, it was impossible to discern exactly how much of her inconsistent rambling could be contributed to the morphine. But there was one thing for which she hoped to get an honest answer. "You said Rocky left town. Where did he go, Mama?"

"I don't know, sugar. He wrote to Cherub, and she ran off to live with him. I had become so conniving that she couldn't stand me. She hates me, Lilah. I'm a mean old woman and I have no right to ask either of you for your forgiveness."

"You don't have to ask, Mama. You're forgiven."

"You won't say that when you hear what an awful thing, Lilah. Find Rocky, Lilah. Don't stop until you find him."

"I will, Mama." Lilah knew her mother wanted her to find Rocky in order to bring Cherie home, but her daughter wasn't the only one she longed to bring home.

"I pray you both can forgive me."

"We do, Mama. You're forgiven."

Dovie was asleep before she finished her statement.

CHAPTER 25

Rocky barely slept all night. Was he doing the right thing, or merely dreaming? Was he really advocating for Dovie Albertson to be living under his roof, after all the years he complained about the woman being in the same house? Yet, how many times had he said if he could turn back the pages, he'd do things differently? Wasn't this his chance? Isn't it what Lilah would've wanted? He couldn't go back in time, but he could keep from making the same mistake twice. Cherie loved her grandmother, but he and Dovie had forced her to choose between them.

Looking out his bedroom window at a quarter-past-five, he could see a light on in the café. He was surprised since the café closed on Sundays. He dressed and rushed over. Becky wiped away tears as she explained that Sam had died in the night, and she was making a wreath with a black ribbon for the front door.

"Rocky, I know it isn't my call, but I can offer advice and what you do with it is up to you. But this entire community will be grieving. Sam was more like a grandfather to us all, and out of respect, I'd suggest closing the doors of The Sam & Sadie for a week. Even if you should choose not to, I don't think we'll have customers. The people here don't come for the food as much as they do for the lighthearted atmosphere as they gather with friends. This week will be a time of mourning."

"I understand and completely agree. When did you get the news?"

"His son called me at four o'clock this morning. I dressed and came on over to make the wreath."

"Could you make a sign for the front door, to let the people know the café will be closed until further notice?"

"A sign won't be necessary. The news will be all over town by noon. I called Pastor Henderson at Mr. Olive Church, and Brother Arnold at Kennesaw Holiness. Both expressed their sorrow and said they'd announce it to their congregations."

Rocky said he and Cherub would wait until after Sam's funeral to leave town. Moisture welled in her eyes. Was she crying for her friend, Sam? Or had he caused the tears? Rocky wanted to hold her in his arms and tell her he loved her. It was the truth. He just didn't love her the way she deserved to be loved. He knew what it felt like to be *in* love, and this wasn't it. Wanting to make up for the pain he caused, he said, "Becky, I'd like for you to go to the bank with me in the morning. I'd like to transfer the deed to the Sam & Sadie into your name."

Her jaw jutted forward. "Rocky, I don't need your charity."

"It's not charity. If it'll make you feel better, then deposit a couple of dollars a week into my account, until it's paid off."

She laughed. "I should be able to handle that . . . *if* I were staying! But Angel and I will be leaving here soon, also."

"You aren't serious."

"Oh, but I am."

"Becky, you can't leave. Kennesaw wouldn't be the same without you. Where would you go?" He stopped to draw a breath and then asked the question he'd been afraid to ask. "Am I the cause of you wanting to run away?"

"Run away? Rocky, this trip was in the works long before you drove into town. The plan all along was to settle in Still Waters after Angel graduated, and that time has come."

"Funny, you never mentioned it until now. Maybe the time has come for your little bird to leave the nest, but that doesn't mean you have to upend your life. Angel is a beautiful, self-sufficient young woman and for years, you've put your life on hold for her sake. Now that she's ready to go off to college, maybe it's time for you to let her try her wings and soar."

"That's the plan. Rocky. I want her to soar. But don't you see? If I stayed here, Angel would come home from college every break. Then, after graduation, she'd return here, work with me in the café, and life would pass her by, just as it has for me. There are no young men in Kennesaw between the ages of eighteen and sixty. As soon as the guys graduate high school, they move away to college or to Atlanta. I need to leave for her sake."

Rocky knew she was right about the men in Kennesaw. Homer Jenkins was probably the youngest adult male, and he celebrated his sixtieth birthday two weeks ago.

Becky said, "I don't wish my life on anyone. I want Angel to fall in love and have a family. It won't happen if I stay here."

Rocky nodded. "Okay, you've convinced me."

She grinned. "I must say, that was a quick change of heart."

"It hit me when you said, 'It won't happen if I stay here.' Becky, Angel isn't the only one who deserves to find happiness. You're a very attractive woman, but you're hid in this little out-of-the-way place. It's not too late for you to find love, but for that to happen, you need to be in a larger town where you can meet eligible men nearer your age. Look at you! You're beautiful, smart, funny, caring . . . you're everything any man could want."

"Not every man, Rocky. I'm not what you want." Hanging her head, she mumbled. "I'm sorry, I shouldn't have said that."

Rocky pondered her statement. She was wrong. Or was she? There was no doubt in his mind that Becky would marry him in a quick minute if only he'd ask. What was stopping him? Lilah was gone. He'd never find another woman to fill the hole in his heart, but if Becky could be happy with him, why shouldn't he give her a home and a family? She'd make a wonderful mother. He couldn't deny that more than once he'd laid awake in bed and fantasized what it would be like.

He looked at her and pictured her pregnant. Biting his lip to keep from smiling, Rocky could only imagine how thrilled she would be to have a child of her own. In her early thirties, it wasn't' too late for it to happen.

Her perfectly shaped lips turned up slightly and her blue eyes twinkled when she caught him staring.

She picked up his coffee cup and walked into the kitchen to refill it. He watched the way she glided around the room, her long hair swaying as she walked, and the way the wide sash fit tightly around her tiny waist. She could pass for twenty-one.

He swallowed hard and tried to clear his head of the utterly ridiculous notion. Had he lost his mind? Giving birth to a child might be a dream come true for her, but he had a daughter, and starting over was not in his life's plans. His heart pounded like a jackhammer, just thinking of how close he could've come to making a monumental mistake.

****

Rocky and Cherie were running late for the funeral, but if he put it off any longer, he might not go through with it. Every time he'd convince himself that going back to Nearby and making amends with Dovie was the right thing to do, he'd suddenly remember a conversation with the old woman that would set his teeth on edge.

It would be different if Cherie was looking forward to going back to make amends with her grandmother. But she wasn't. Maybe he wouldn't feel inclined to insist, if he didn't know the reason she wanted to stay was because of the boy at the party who had her snowed. True, he and Lilah were in love at Cherie's age, but then they were more mature at sixteen. Weren't they?

She walked in the room holding her gloves in her hand. "Daddy the funeral starts in fifteen minutes. I'm sure the church will be crowded. Shouldn't we leave?"

"You're right, honey, but there's something we need to discuss." He groped for the right words. How would Lilah want him to handle the situation? He knew Cherie couldn't possibly be in love, after being with the fellow only one time, but since she was convinced, it was crucial he handle the situation the right way.

"Cherie, I think you and I should go to back to Alabama, but I understand you want to stay in Georgia. So, I'd like to propose a deal."

"Fine. You go to Nearby, Daddy, and I'll stay in Kennesaw, and we can both live happily ever after. Deal?"

His voice cracked. "Honey, if you think I could ever be happy without you in my life, you don't know me."

"Oh, Daddy, I'm sorry. I didn't mean it. I could never be happy without you, either. What kind of deal?"

"We'll stay in Kennesaw as long as Bobby is in town, but—"

She blushed. "His name is Billy."

"Sorry! Billy. But when he goes back home, then give him your grandmother's address, so he can write to you in Nearby."

She teared up. "I thought you wanted me to live with you."

"I do. I plan to build us a house in Nearby with a mother-in-law suite. Dovie could have her own private living quarters, separated from our part of the house by a covered breezeway.. Your grandmother is all alone, and there'll likely come a day when she'll need us. We're the only family she has."

Cherie playfully reached up and touched his forehead with the back of her hand. "Daddy, do you have a fever? You're talking out of your head."

"You don't approve?"

"Are you kidding? Nothing would make me happier than for you and Big Mama to stop the feuding, but even if you were serious, she'd never go for it. I love her, and I feel guilty for leaving her, but you both forced me to make a choice. When I'm with her, I miss you, but when I'm with you, I miss her."

"Well, I was wrong. You shouldn't have to choose."

"That would make me happy—but you two living under the same roof? That's a disaster waiting to happen."

"I didn't try before. I'm ready to make it work. I know you've enjoyed the last few weeks here, with Angel, but you realize she'll be leaving for college soon. I'm afraid you might get lonesome."

"Yikes! You're right. It would be terribly lonely here with you both gone." She sighed. "I'm sorry I gave you a hard time, Daddy. Going home is the right thing to do. When should we tell Angel and Becky?"

"It's no secret. I've already discussed it with Becky, so she won't be surprised. She may have shared it with Angel by now, but if not, you can tell her after the funeral. Speaking of the funeral, we'd better hurry."

Going back to Nearby made sense on so many levels, but Cherub supposed it meant giving up on the beautiful plan she and Angel concocted to get her daddy and Becky together.

****

Tuesday morning, August 12, 1957, Mt. Olive Church in Kennesaw was filled to overflowing. The funeral home handed out cardboard fans, with their advertising on the back and a picture of Jesus with the little children on the front. Or maybe it was the other way around, but no one appeared to care what was printed on either side, as they swished them back and forth on one of the hottest days of the year.

Rocky and Cherie tiptoed inside the church and saw Becky and Angel sitting next to the last seat on the left. Becky motioned for them and pointed to the seat beside her. They slid over, assuring Rocky that there was plenty of room.

Hazel sang Beulah Land, and the Journey Brothers Quartet, made up of Leonard, Max and Lloyd sang Precious Memories. It was the standard request at every funeral. Sam was the one who started the quartet, but when he became too ill to sing, the other three refused to replace their beloved bass singer. Neither did they want to change the name from a quartet to the Journey Brothers Trio, since it would mean omitting the one who was instrumental in leading all three to the Lord. Leonard said every time someone commented that it took four to make a quartet, it was an opportunity to tell them of their salvation story.

Pastor Henderson delivered a beautiful eulogy, befitting the deceased, but one person after another walked up to the pulpit with their own story to tell of how Sam had impacted their life.

After the closing prayer, the preacher announced that the Women's Quarterly Meeting had fixed lunch in the Fellowship Hall and everyone was invited. He said, "Tables are set up, but since we have such a huge crowd, some of you may wish to take your plates outside and eat under the big oak."

Becky said, "I don't know about the rest of you, but I'd much rather eat outside. It won't be nearly as hot under the shade as it will be in that packed room."

Rocky agreed, and it didn't appear the girls cared where they sat, as long as they were together. Before they had time to finish lunch, Cherie broke the ice and shared with Angel that she and her father were planning to move.

Rocky's heart ached when he saw the girls hugging with tears seeping down their cheeks.

Angel said, "What will I do? Cherie, you're the best friend I've ever had. In fact, you're the only friend I've ever had."

Cherie teared up. "But that's not true, Angel. You were President of the Student body at your school. Everyone loves you."

"I have lots of acquaintances, but only one true friend."

"What about Bobby?"

"He's sweet, but he doesn't know me the way you do. You make me feel normal."

"But you *are* normal."

"Good try, but I'm blind and that's all that some people ever get to know about me. It's considered a 'handicap,' for a reason."

"Everyone has a handicap, Angel. In my case, it's self-inflicted. I hold grudges when someone hurts my feelings, even though I know it's wrong. Not you. You're very forgiving. The other day, Mrs. Crenshaw talked to you as if being blind equates with incompetence. Yet you smiled and thanked her. How do you do it? I wanted to give her a piece of my mind."

She laughed. "I'm used to it. Besides, it's usually kids who are just curious, or elderly people like Mrs. Crenshaw, who mean no harm. I'm not offended."

"That's what I'm saying. I would be, and I'd be slow to forgive. I want to be more like you." She giggled. "I think we've just learned which of us has the better friend, and it's me. My friend is blind, but your friend is stubborn and unforgiving."

Angel's lip quivered as she reached out her arms for a hug. "I'll miss you."

Rocky's heart broke seeing the girls crying. He said, "I've just had an idea, Becky, and please hear me out before nixing it. Since the café will be closed all week in memory of Sam, why don't you and Cherie ride down with us this afternoon and let us acquaint you with the little town of Nearby."

Cherie squealed, "Oh, Daddy, that's a great idea."

Becky frowned. "I don't know, Rocky. Wouldn't it be better

for us all to say our goodbyes now, rather than dragging it out?"

His throat tightened. Was she thinking of the girls or was she referring to their relationship? He couldn't deny that there were feelings there. He'd definitely miss her. Would he live out the remainder of his days with regrets for what might have been?

The girls jumped up and down and squealed as if they'd been offered the moon. Becky looked at Rocky and nodded. "Okay. It looks as if we're going. I'll go home and pack a few things. What time would you like to leave?"

He glanced at his watch. "It's twelve-thirty. Could you be ready by two o'clock?"

"Sure. Angel and I will stay a couple of days, then take the bus back home. It'll be my first vacation in over twelve years."

"Then you're due a road trip. I'll pick you girls up at two."

CHAPTER 26

The trip back to Nearby didn't seem nearly as long to Rocky as it did the day he left there and wound up on the road to Kennesaw, last March. But there were several things that could account for it. That particular night, he was literally out of his head with grief, after learning of Lilah's death, Although he'd never stop missing her, his heart felt lightened by the giggling coming from the back seat. It felt good to see his daughter happy. Not only that, but he felt rather pleased with himself that he thought to invite Becky. Twelve years without a vacation was twelve years too long.

Cherub leaned forward, looking out the window. "You're taking me to Big Mama's?"

"Didn't you say you'd like to make amends?"

"Yessir, but not yet. I want to spend as much time at the hotel with Angel as I can, before she has to go back to Kennesaw."

"Sweetheart, you'll have that chance. I've booked rooms for all of us at the Osceola Hotel. Angel and Becky have plans to stay

THE ROAD TO KENNESAW

for a few days. But before your grandmother hears that we're in town and gets her dander up, we need to go by and make our peace with her."

"But Daddy, you know how she is. She'll be furious. Why don't we wait until Becky and Angel leave, then go over and give her a chance to let off steam. There's no need in subjecting them to one of Big Mama's tirades, and this one is bound to be a doozy."

"Honey, your concerns are valid, but I believe this is the right thing to do. The minute we stop to eat, someone will see us and call to tell her we're in town. It's better this way."

Rocky pulled up in front of the farmhouse. Becky said, "Angel and I will wait in the car."

He laughed. "I suppose we've scared you, but you might as well come in. It'll be hot out here. Besides, you aren't the ones she's angry with. You'll find out that Dovie loves everybody . . . everybody except me."

Becky grinned. "I'm sure that's not true."

Cherub said, "It was true until I ran away. Now, I'm sure she doesn't like me, either."

Rocky parked the car, then went around to open Becky's door.

Just before reaching the doorsteps, he looked up, then stopped short in his tracks. Could it be the heat? He jerked his handkerchief from his hip pocket and blotted his forehead. He blinked several times, but the outline of the image behind the screen door remained. His pulse raced. It couldn't be Lilah. Lilah was dead.

Cherie let out a scream as she ran up the steps. "Mama? Is it really you?"

Hugging her daughter, Lilah's tears flowed. "Yes, my sweet baby, it's me."

"But you died . . . or that's what they told me."

"So I've heard. It's a long story."

Lilah saw Rocky standing behind their daughter with a beautiful young woman. Her heart shattered into a million pieces. Why was she surprised? Regardless of whether he heard she was dead, or whether he was told she went on a cruise with Coot, he would have no reason to wait around and hope for a reconciliation. Attempting to hide the hurt, she said, "Hello, Rocky. It's good to see you. Please introduce me to your friend."

"Lilah, we were told you were dead."

"Well, as you can see, the rumors of my death have been greatly exaggerated." She attempted to smile, but her lips wouldn't cooperate.

He bungled through an introduction that left Becky feeling she should have stayed home.

After introducing her friend, Angel, Cherie said, "Mama, we have so much to talk about. Where have you been? Why did you let us think you were dead? Don't you even care what we went through?"

"I'm sorry, honey, but you don't understand."

"Then explain."

"I promise I will, sweetheart, but this is not the time. Later."

Becky said, "It's nice to meet you, Mrs. Stone, but Angel and I will wait outside and allow you and your family time together. After Rocky visits with you mother, he can take us to the bus station, and we'll be on our way home."

"There's no reason for you to sit in the heat. Please come inside. Rocky, I hope you'll go in and speak to Mama. She's had a stroke, but she's been asking for you."

Rocky raised a brow. "I'm sure she has. Is the shotgun loaded?"

She smiled. "She'll be pleased to see you, but I'm warning you, she's on morphine and she's not making much sense."

Rocky sucked in a lungful of air. "If she's asking to see me, then I know for sure that she's out of her head. Come on, ladies, we're all going in together. I need backup."

When they walked into the room, Lilah said, "Mama, you have visitors."

Dovie opened her eyes, glared, then with arms opened wide, she burst into shouts of joy. "Hallelujah! Thank you, Lord, thank you, Lord, thank you, Lord."

Cherie ran and hugged her grandmother. "I've missed you, Big Mama. I'm so sorry for not letting you know where I was. I shouldn't have run away." Dovie clasped both hands around her granddaughter's face. "Shush, sweet girl. Don't you cry. You did what you needed to do."

Dovie turned and set her eyes on Rocky, and in a soft voice he hardly recognized, she patted the mattress. "Come, sit on the bed beside, me Rocky. I prayed that you'd return before the Lord called me home, and my prayers have been answered."

He glanced at Lilah, who lifted both shoulders and grinned.

This was not how Rocky had imagined the meeting would go. He eased down on the side of the bed. Wringing his hands together, he said, "Dovie, I want to apologize for the unkind things I've said to you and about you through the years. I was wrong." Even if she couldn't fully comprehend, he had to say it.

She chuckled. Not the smirky chuckle he'd learn to recognize from years of living with the woman, but there was a strange, cordial sound to it—or at least strange and cordial coming from the mother-in-law who hated him.

"You're being too kind, Rocky. We both know I was an ornery ol' cuss, and you should've kicked me out of the house years ago. But I have a confession to make to you and my daughter."

Dovie reached for a glass of water sitting on the bedside table. Rocky handed it to her, then held the straw while she sipped a few swallows. She thanked him. Then closing her eyes, she said, "To quote Betty Davis, 'Fasten your seatbelt, it's gonna be a bumpy night.'"

He looked up at Cherie, who stood next to him, and lifted his shoulders. Had the old lady lost it? What was she referring to?

Dovie said, "Rocky, I should've told you this long ago. I'm so sorry."

"It's okay, Big Mama. You can tell me now."

"You were off fighting a war when Lilah went into labor. You had no way of knowing, but my daughter almost died, giving birth to the twins."

Rocky knew the old woman was talking out of her head, but he went along with her. Besides, he liked the new Dovie. "Ah, yes. The twins."

Her words came out in spurts. "You think I'm just a crazy old lady . . . and don't know what I'm saying . . . but I'm trying to tell you and Lilah what I should've told you sixteen years ago. Lilah gave birth to two beautiful little girls. I'm so very, very sorry to have kept it from you."

Rocky was taken aback by the wild admission. He said, "It's okay, Big Mama. You've told us now, so try to rest."

He expected Dovie to insist she wasn't his Big Mama. He almost wished she would. Her out-of-character mild manner was offsetting.

Dovie's voice trembled. "All these years you thought I hated you, Rocky. I didn't hate you. I hated the fact that you were a constant reminder of my dark secret. I loathed myself, and I took my anger out on you."

Never in a lifetime would Rocky have thought he'd ever feel sorry for Dovie Albertson, but then he'd never seen this soft side of her. "It's okay, Dovie. I forgive you, and I pray that you can forgive me for all the times I've wronged you." It was what he'd gone there to say, yet he would've felt better if she'd been in the right frame of mind to understand.

The old woman went into full-blown sobs. "You don't understand. I don't deserve your forgiveness. You aren't listening to me."

Lilah said, "Say what you feel you need to say, Mama. We promise to listen."

Dovie grasped Lilah's hands. "Oh, my darling daughter, you will hate me when you learn what I have done, and you'll have every right."

"Nothing could make me hate you Mama."

"You will, honey. You both will. But I can't face Jesus with this on my conscience." She closed her eyes, as she began to speak. "Lilah, you went through labor for eighteen long hours. I was terrified that I'd lose you. You were in awful pain."

Lilah smiled. "That I haven't forgotten."

"I was glad when the midwife administered ether, but it rendered you unconscious when the girls were born. The midwife took them into the bathroom and cleaned them up. It was a difficult delivery, and I began to worry if you'd ever wake up, but the babies were beautiful. If only—"

Rocky's gaze locked with Lilah's.

CHAPTER 27

As much as Rocky wanted to believe Dovie was talking out of her head, he found it difficult to completely dismiss the irrational babbling. No way could she have kept such a horrific secret bottled inside for sixteen years. Could she? Then again, didn't it sound like something the conniving, manipulative old woman that he had known through the years could do? What if? He licked his lips, and in a slow, controlled tone, he said, "Dovie, think hard about what you're saying. I think you're confused. You aren't trying to say that we lost a baby when Cherub was born. Are you?"

With her lips pressed together in a straight white line, she gave a weak nod. "A beautiful baby girl. I'm so sorry. It's haunted me for years. I'm glad the truth is out before going to my grave."

Throwing up his hands, he yelled, "Why you vindictive old woman. Why are we just now being told?"

Becky tugged on his sleeve and whispered. "Rocky, it might be wise to calm down. She's on morphine."

He jerked away. "She'd better hope it's the morphine." He ran his hand across the back of his neck. "Okay, Dovie, if Lilah gave birth to twins, what did you do with our baby? Did you bury her in an obscure field someplace? Or did you just toss her in the trash? Did you do away with her because of your hatred for me?"

Lilah said, "Becky's right, Rocky. The stroke has affected Mama's mind. This is something she's dreamed up and believes to be true. We didn't have a baby to die."

Dovie said, "I never said she died."

Throwing up his hands, Rocky said, "Then where is she?"

"Poor little creature had a terrible birth defect that would require constant care for the rest of her life. Lilah was in no shape to handle the truth, so it was left up to me to decide what to do with the child. I did what I thought was best at the time."

"Are you saying you put her in an institution?"

"No, it didn't come to that."

"Don't you dare die without telling me what you did with my baby."

Cherie whispered, "Daddy, you're being harsh. Big Mama is telling you what she believes to be true. I think she dreamed it. It hurts me to hear you fussing at her."

He nodded. "Sorry, baby. I hope you're right, and it was a dream, but I have to know the truth."

Dovie said, "No one but the good Lord knows how many times I've hated myself every day since making that decision. But I had listened to my daughter scream in pain for hours on end, until I was about crazy. I wanted to help her, yet there was nothing I could do. When the midwife told me the child would need care for the rest of her life, I lost my head. I was worried that Lilah was about to die, and even if she lived, Rocky, I was afraid you'd be killed, and she wouldn't be able to care for two babies—especially since one would require constant care. I asked the midwife to take her to the State Welfare Department. I knew they'd see she got proper care." Then, closing her eyes as if she had completed her mission, she said, "Please excuse me. I'm tired. So very tired."

Afraid she would die before getting the information he so desperately wanted, Rocky made a concentrated effort to keep his tone subdued for Cherie's sake. But he had to know. "Dovie, please. Just one more thing. I don't suppose you know where I can find this midwife?"

Without opening her eyes, she mumbled. "Dead. . . baby with granddaughter."

Angel whispered, "Cherie, when is your birthday?"

"April 4th."

"Mine, too." Then hurriedly pushing her way up to the bed, Angel touched the mattress, the pillow, then patted Dovie's hair and gently stroked it with her hand. "I forgive you, Big Mama."

With her eyes still closed, Dovie reached for her hand and kissed it. Tears rolled down her wrinkled, pale cheeks. "Thank you, Cherie, but I don't deserve your forgiveness, sweetheart."

"I'm not Cherie, Big Mama. I'm Cherie's twin. My name is

Angel."

Lilah whispered, "You're very sweet, Angel, but my mother is sick and doesn't know what she's saying."

Becky said, "Oh, but she knows exactly what she's saying. I am the midwife's granddaughter. My grandmother told me she lived in a town nearby when the twins were born to a woman whose husband was fighting in the war. I understood her to mean she lived in the same vicinity as the twins' mother. Now, I realize she was saying Nearby was the name of the town. Lilah and Rocky, meet your daughter, Angel."

Rocky glared at Lilah. "Could this be true? Twins?"

"Impossible. Mama couldn't have possibly given away my baby."

Becky said, "Of course, it's true, Rocky. Lilah's mother told it exactly the way my grandmother told it to me. The only difference was I thought it was the mother's idea. I know now it was the grandmother's decision."

Lilah threw her arms around Angel, showering her with kisses. "My baby? Oh, Angel, my beautiful daughter, I knew nothing of this. When I was carrying you girls, the midwife said I looked as if I might have twins. But when I woke up and I only had one baby, I assumed the excess weight was caused by toxemia. If I had known, I would've found you, sweetheart, even if I'd had to look the world over."

"Don't feel sorry for me. I've had a wonderful life, and now to find out that my mother isn't dead, I have a father and the best twin sister I could ever hope for, I'd say I'm a very blessed girl."

Cherie squealed, "Isn't this the wildest thing? Twins. I want to be angry with Big Mama for keeping us apart, but I'm too happy at the moment to be angry."

Lilah took Dovie by the hand. "Mama? Can you hear me?" There was no answer.

Becky whispered, "Rocky, I think someone should call her doctor. Does anyone know his number?"

Lilah said, "I know how to reach him."

Rocky flinched. "I'm sure you do." He hadn't had time to ponder where Lilah had been during the time he believed her to be dead. Now, he didn't have to ask. Dovie finally got her wish. He had mourned for Lilah when he thought she was dead. But now, feeling dead inside, he mourned for himself.

Coot arrived in less than ten minutes and asked everyone to clear the room. Shortly afterward,, he opened the door and ushered them all back in.

Cherub walked up to the bedside and sobbed softly. Angel said, "Our Big Mama is dead. Isn't she?"

Lilah reached for her hand. "Yes, sweetheart. But the Lord answered her prayer. She lived to see you and to know that she was forgiven before walking through Heaven's gate. It's evident she suffered greatly for her mistake, but she's finally at peace."

Coot called for an ambulance, then walked out on the porch where the family had gathered.

Lilah said, "Coot, I'd like to introduce you to Rocky's friend, Becky, and our daughter, Angel."

"Your what?"

"It's a long story with a beautiful ending. Angel, this is Dr. Sebastian Culpepper, known to those near and dear to him as Coot. Your daddy and I grew up with him. He's been a great friend—"

Rocky threw his cap in the air and shouted, "That's right. Yes! Yes! We are!"

Angel laughed. "Goodness! You and Dr. Coot must be very close."

"What? Dr. who?" He grabbed Angel in a hug. "It wasn't until Lilah said, 'Your daddy and I,' that reality set in. I'm your daddy, Angel!"

Cherie laughed. "Daddy, are you alright?"

"I'm more than alright. I'm ecstatic. I was so caught up in the whole twisted story of Lilah having a baby to be snatched away, that I couldn't get past the anger long enough to absorb the news that our missing baby was found. But it took a little longer to put it together that she's standing here with us. I'm your daddy, Angel."

Angel hugged her father. "Someone please tell me this isn't a dream."

Lilah said, "I feel the same way, sweetheart." Then looking around, she said, "Where is Coot?"

Rocky said, "I think he left. But where's Becky?"

Angel said, "She left with Dr. Coot. She said he wanted to show her the clinic, but they'd be back shortly."

Lilah clasped her hands under her chin. "Oh, m'goodness, wouldn't that be grand?"

Cherie giggled, "Mama, you don't really think—do you? How funny!"

Rocky shrugged. "What's going on?

Lilah said, "Open your eyes, Rocky. Didn't you notice the way Coot looked at Becky? He's definitely enamored with her. I watched them interacting and she was literally glowing."

"Don't be silly. You're making it up."

"Why would I make it up? Becky truly is beautiful and seems genuinely sweet. Wouldn't they be perfect together?"

Rocky said, "But I thought you . . . and Coot?"

"You thought wrong. Besides I'm a married woman, and my husband is very jealous. Do you think Becky might be persuaded to stay in Nearby?"

"Not a chance. I had to talk her into coming here for a visit. She'll be heading for a town called Still Waters, after leaving here."

"Oh, drats. I was hoping—Coot needs a sweet woman in his life. Did you say she's moving to Sweet Water? I have a cousin there."

"No. Still Waters."

"Never heard of it. Is it in Georgia?"

"I assume that it is, although I haven't looked it up on the map."

Cherie said, "Angel, I can't wait for you to meet our other grandmother, Granny Stone. She's a hoot. You'll love her."

Lilah said, "Cherie is right. Your Granny Stone is a sweet, fun lady. She loves to take Cherie shopping and now she'll have twice the fun. Why don't we all go inside? It's much cooler in the house. The attic fan does a good job of keeping it comfortable. Besides, I could use your help in planning Big Mama's funeral."

After thirty minutes going over arrangements, such as notifying the preacher, the organist, the singer, what songs to be sung, and what dress to send to the funeral home for Big Mama, Coot and Becky came walking in laughing like a couple of teenagers. Coot handed Lilah a sack full of chili dogs and fries. He said, "Becky and I figured everyone would be getting hungry by now, so we stopped at a little drive-in called The Grill and picked up supper."

Lilah glanced around. "Where did Becky go?"

Coot said, "She walked outside with Angel. They'll be in shortly."

Angel came back in smiling. She whispered to Cherie, "I have great news, sister, but I'll wait and let Becky share it."

Cherie giggled. "I can hardly wait to hear. Sister!"

Rocky's heart melted, watching his daughters. He realized for the first time that Angel favored Lilah even more than Cherub. Why had he not noticed the resemblance before?

Cherie reached in the cabinet for plates and handed a few to Angel. "I'll set out the silverware if you'll pour the tea. The glasses are on the counter to the right of the refrigerator. The refrigerator is—"

Angel said, "I know where it is. I found it earlier."

Lilah watched as her blind daughter waltzed over to the fridge, opened the door and took out two ice trays. She cracked them open and filled the glasses as if she had twenty-twenty vision.

Everyone gathered around the table and Coot said "Before we eat, I'd like to share some great news. I have a new assistant, and I couldn't be more thrilled."

Angel whispered to Cherie, "That's my good news. I haven't known Becky to be this excited in a long time."

Rocky ran his hand back of his neck. Looking at Becky, he said, "I don't suppose he's referring to you, since you have no experience as a physician's assistant?"

Coot said, "I can teach her what she needs to know."

Becky smiled. "Isn't it great?"

"I don't know. Is it? What about Still Waters? I thought you were eager to go there."

"I was. Thank you for bringing me."

"I don't get it."

Lilah smiled. "I think I do, and it's exciting. We'd love to hear, Becky, if you don't mind sharing."

The twins clapped and yelled, "Speech, speech!"

Becky bit her lip, then glanced at Coot and smiled. "Oh my, where should I begin? What a bitter-sweet day this has been. It's the day you all lost a mother, grandmother and friend . . . the day a woman who spent years grieving over a past sin, made her peace with her family and her Lord, before taking her last breath . . . My sweet Angel has found her way home . . . Rocky and Lilah are together . . . the doctor has filled a needed position at the clinic. . . and I have been brought to this place by divine appointment. Truly, this is the day that the Lord has made."

Rocky grunted, but a chorus of 'Amens,' along with 'Let us rejoice and be glad in it,' drowned out his skepticism. He was torn between what he should do and what he wanted to do. Becky moving to Nearby and working for Coot Culpepper would be a huge mistake, and he wanted to tell her so. But was it his place?

Clearing his voice, he said, "I agree it's been quite a day. Now, before our lunch gets cold, let's pray and enjoy these chili dogs."

Becky lifted her hand slightly. "I'd like to lead the prayer, if you don't mind. Feel free to join in." Heads bowed as she began quoting the twenty-third Psalm. "The Lord is my Shepherd, I shall not want. He maketh me to lie down in green pastures; He leadeth me beside the still waters. He restoreth my soul . . ."

Rocky didn't hear the remainder, since his thoughts were stuck on the Still Waters.

Becky walked out on the porch with her hot dog and sat in the swing. He sat down beside her and whispered, "I hope you know what you're doing and didn't allow Coot to sway you. He can be very persistent. Nearby is a neat little town, and it's larger than

Kennesaw, but it's not what you're looking for, Becky."

"Oh, but it's exactly what I've been looking for, even when I didn't know where to find it. I've never been so sure of anything in my life, Rocky. Don't you get it? This is the town where my grandmother began her career as a midwife and rescued a sweet little blind baby. It's no coincidence that Angel and I found our way back here today."

"I'll admit, it does seem rather odd, but I'd be slow to call it divine intervention. I wish I could be happy for you, but since I'm the one who brought you here, I don't want to be the cause of you making a huge mistake."

"Oh, Rocky, I'm trying to tell you that you aren't the reason I'm in Nearby. God led me to this place for such a time as this. Years ago, I heard a preacher preach on Psalms 42, and I knew it was meant for me. 'As a hart pants for the water brook, so my soul pants for God.'"

"You lost me after your panting heart."

"H-a-r-t, hart. The psalmist is describing a deer, seeking the place to quench his thirst. Then, after reading the twenty-third Psalm one night. I underlined two words—still waters. I marked the date in the left column. June 25, 1953. I've waited, knowing when the time was right, the Lord would lead me to my water brook. I won't say I didn't get impatient at times, but I never stopped believing that it would happen in His time. I've known all along that Kennesaw was a pit stop and not my destination. When you drove into Nearby today, even though I had never been here, I knew I was home. God has brought me to my still waters—and my soul has been restored."

"Becky, face it, you needed a vacation. The euphoria you're feeling is what we all feel when we get away from the stress of everyday life. You're here because Sam died, the restaurant would be closed for a week, and I encouraged you to come because you needed a break. Don't try twisting the truth to fit what you want to believe."

"Are you saying you don't believe in prayer?"

"I'll just say my track record isn't very good: For years I prayed for Dovie to move back to the farm."

Becky said, "The farm? Where is the farm?"

"Well, it's . . ." He shrugged and glanced around him. "Well, it's here, but—" He grinned. "Okay, so she moved back, but not because of answered prayer. I'm the one who made it happen. I loaded up her things on a truck and brought them here."

"So, is that when you stopped believing in prayer?"

"No. Call me a slow learner. I prayed desperately for God to put Lilah back into my—" Before he could finish his sentence, Lilah walked up and handed him a glass of sweet tea.

Becky smiled. "You were saying?"

"Okay, I know what you're thinking. But look how long it took and all that we went through."

"But you *are* back together. So, how did you wind up in Kennesaw? Another answered prayer?"

He laughed. "Not hardly. It was a fluke. I'd never even heard of the place. Believing Lilah was dead, I lost my head. I got in the car and drove with no destination in mind. I have no idea how I wound up on the road to Kennesaw. The only reason I stopped there was because it was late, and I was exhausted."

She laughed. "And you don't think God led you there for such a time as this?"

He tried to hide his aggravation. "You keep saying that, but I have no idea what it even means. Look, I'm glad the prayer thing works for you, Becky, but apparently I'm not one of God's favorites."

"Rocky, God has kept you in the palm of His hand, even when you've tried to pull away. He's answered every prayer and used every event to lead you to this particular place at this particular time, where you and Lilah would meet the daughter you never knew you had."

That night, Rocky found it impossible to fall asleep. Was it the three hot dogs he had for supper, the thought of Becky falling prey to Coot's charm, or the Psalm he learned in Sunday School when he was eight years old? *The Lord is my shepherd, I shall not want. He maketh me to lie down in green pastures; He leadeth me beside the still waters. He restoreth my soul.* He pictured the Shepherd, leading Becky, His beloved lamb, to drink of the still waters in Nearby. Realizing all the anger and bitterness he'd harbored for years was gone, he prayed, "Thank you Lord for your grace and mercy, when I deserved neither. Truly, my soul has been restored." Feeling a burden he bore for years had been lifted, he drifted off to a peaceful sleep.

****

Westview Church in Nearby was packed the morning of Dovie Albertson's funeral. The four ladies on the Benevolence Committee, Mrs. Ouzts, Mrs. Reagan, Mrs. Hatcher and Mrs. Messer invited everyone to stay for lunch after the funeral.

Rocky and Lilah walked outside with their plates, sat on the grass away from the crowd, and discussed a future he couldn't have fathomed a week ago. His heart overflowed with emotion. He had his family back. But would Angel want to be with them or stay with Becky? Seeing the twins together, it was obvious they wouldn't choose to be separated again. He and Lilah agreed it had to be the girls' choice, not theirs.

Lilah asked Rocky to tell her all about Kennesaw and the friends he met there. Before he finished, she gushed, "Oh, Rocky! Let's make it our home."

"You aren't serious."

"Why not? You already own an apartment and café there, and I can't wait to meet your friends--especially the Duvall sisters."

He laughed. "I couldn't run the cafe without Becky, sweetheart, but God has led her to her still waters. Besides, the café was there when I needed it, but it's not what I'd choose to do for the rest of my life. While you were in the hospital, I had an opportunity to buy a ranch, but the timing wasn't right."

"A ranch? Oh, m'goodness, honey, you'd make a great rancher. We'll sell the café and search for suitable pastureland around Kennesaw, if that's what you want."

"Sounds perfect."

"Then why are you laughing?"

"I'm picturing us lying down in our green pastures. I ask you, honey . . .with the Lord as my Shepherd, what more could I want?"

www.ingramcontent.com/pod-product-compliance
Lightning Source LLC
Chambersburg PA
CBHW050356260626
47156CB00003B/755